# YUKIO MISHIMA

# The Sound of Waves

Yukio Mishima was born into a samurai family and imbued with the code of complete control over mind and body, and loyalty to the Emperor—the same code that produced the austerity and self-sacrifice of Zen. He wrote countless short stories and thirty-three plays, in some of which he acted. Several films have been made from his novels, including *The Sound of Waves; Enjo,* which was based on *The Temple of the Golden Pavilion;* and *The Sailor Who Fell from Grace with the Sea.* Among his other works are the novels *Confessions of a Mask* and *Thirst for Love* and the short-story collections *Death in Midsummer* and *Acts of Worship.*

*The Sea of Fertility* tetralogy (available in its entirety in Vintage International), however, is his masterpiece. After Mishima conceived the idea of *The Sea of Fertility* in 1964, he frequently said he would die when it was completed. "The title, *The Sea of Fertility,*" he told Donald Keene, "is intended to suggest the arid sea of the moon that belies its name. Or I might say that it superimposes the image of cosmic nihilism on that of the fertile sea."

On November 25, 1970, the day he completed *The Decay of the Angel,* the last novel of the cycle, Mishima committed *seppuku* (ritual suicide) at the age of 45.

INTERNATIONAL

BOOKS BY YUKIO MISHIMA

*The Sea of Fertility, a Cycle of Four Novels:*

*Spring Snow*

*Runaway Horses*

*The Temple of Dawn*

*The Decay of the Angel*

*Confessions of a Mask*

*Thirst for Love*

*Forbidden Colors*

*The Sailor Who Fell from Grace with the Sea*

*After the Banquet*

*The Temple of the Golden Pavilion*

*Five Modern Nō Plays*

*The Sound of Waves*

*Death in Midsummer*

*Acts of Worship*

# The Sound of Waves

# YUKIO MISHIMA

VINTAGE INTERNATIONAL

*Vintage Books*

*A Division of Random House, Inc.*

*New York*

# The Sound of Waves

TRANSLATED BY *Meredith Weatherby*

DRAWINGS BY *Yoshinori Kinoshita*

FIRST VINTAGE INTERNATIONAL EDITION, OCTOBER 1994

*Copyright © 1956 by Alfred A. Knopf, Inc.*
*Copyright renewed 1984 by Meredith Weatherby*

All rights reserved under International and Pan-American
Copyright Conventions. Published in the United States by
Vintage Books, a division of Random House, Inc., New York,
and simultaneously in Canada by Random House of Canada Limited,
Toronto. Originally published in Japan as *Shiosai*. This edition
first published in the United States in hardcover by Alfred
A. Knopf, Inc., New York, in 1956.

Library of Congress Cataloging-in-Publication Data
Mishima, Yukio, 1925–1970.
[Shiosai. English]
The sound of waves / by Yukio Mishima ; translated by Meredith
Weatherby ; drawings by Yoshinori Kinoshita.
p.   cm.
ISBN 0-679-75268-4
I. Weatherby, Meredith. II. Kinoshita, Yoshinori, 1898–
PL833.I7S413   1994
895.6' 35 — dc20     94-19314
CIP

Manufactured in the United States of America
E9876543210

# The Sound of Waves

# 1

Uta-jima—Song Island—has only about fourteen hundred inhabitants and a coastline of something under three miles.

The island has two spots with surpassingly beautiful views. One is Yashiro Shrine, which faces northwest and stands near the crest of the island. The shrine commands an uninterrupted view of the wide expanse of the Gulf of Ise, and the island lies directly in the straits connecting the gulf with the Pacific Ocean. The Chita Peninsula approaches from the north, and the Atsumi Peninsula stretches away to the northeast. To the west you can catch glimpses of the coastline between the ports of Uji-Yamada and Yokkaichi in Tsu.

By climbing the two hundred stone steps that lead up to the shrine and looking back from the spot where there is a *torii* guarded by a pair of stone temple-dogs, you can see how these distant shores cradle within their arms the storied Gulf of Ise, unchanged through the centuries. Once there were two *"torii"* pines growing here, their branches twisted and trained into the shape of a *torii*, providing a curious frame for the view, but they died some years ago.

Just now the needles of the surrounding pine trees are still dull-green from winter, but already the spring sea-weeds are staining the sea red near the shore. The north-west monsoon blows steadily from the direction of Tsu, making it still too cold to enjoy the view.

Yashiro Shrine is dedicated to Watatsumi-no-Mikoto, god of the sea. This is an island of fishermen and it is nat-ural that the inhabitants should be devout worshippers of this god. They are forever praying for calm seas, and the very first thing they do upon being rescued from some peril of the sea is to make a votive offering at the sea-god's shrine.

The shrine possesses a treasure of some sixty-six bronze mirrors. One is a grape-design mirror from the eighth century. Another is an ancient copy of a Chinese mirror of the Six Dynasties period, of which there are not more than fifteen or sixteen in all Japan; the deer and squirrels carved on its back must have emerged centuries ago from some Persian forest and journeyed halfway around the earth, across wide continents and endless seas, to come finally to rest here on Uta-jima.

The other most beautiful view on the island is from the lighthouse near the summit of Mt. Higashi, which falls in a cliff to the sea. At the foot of the cliff the current of the Irako Channel sets up an unceasing roar. On windy days these narrow straits connecting the Gulf of Ise and the

Pacific are filled with whirlpools. The tip of the Atsumi Peninsula juts out from across the channel, and on its rocky and desolate shore stands the tiny, unmanned beacon of Cape Irako. Southeast from the Uta-jima lighthouse you can see the Pacific, and to the northeast, across Atsumi Bay and beyond the mountain ranges, you can sometimes see Mt. Fuji, say at dawn when the west wind is blowing strong.

When a steamship sailing to or from Nagoya or Yokka-ichi passed through the Irako Channel, threading its way among the countless fishing-boats scattered the length of the channel between the gulf and the open sea, the lighthouse watchman could easily read its name through his telescope. The *Tokachi-maru,* a Mitsui Line freighter of nineteen hundred tons, had just come within telescopic range. The watchman could see two sailors dressed in gray work-clothes, talking and stamping their feet on the deck. Presently an English freighter, the *Talisman,* sailed into the channel, bound for port. The watchman saw the sailors clearly, looking very tiny as they played quoits on the deck.

The watchman turned to the desk in the watchhouse and, in a log marked "Record of Shipping Movements," entered the vessels' names, signal marks, sailing directions, and the time. Then he tapped this information out on a telegraph key, warning cargo owners in the ports of destination to begin their preparations.

It was afternoon and the sinking sun had been cut off by Mt. Higashi, throwing the vicinity of the lighthouse into shadow. A hawk was circling in the bright sky over the sea. High in the heavens, the hawk was dipping now

5

one wing and then the other, as though testing them, and, just when it seemed about to plummet downward, instead it suddenly slipped backward on the air, and then soared upward again on motionless wings.

After the sun had completely set, a young fisherman came hurrying up the mountain path leading from the village past the lighthouse. He was dangling a large fish in one hand.

The boy was only eighteen, having finished high school just last year. He was tall and well-built beyond his years, and only his face revealed his youthfulness. Skin can be burned no darker by the sun than his was burned. He had the well-shaped nose characteristic of the people of his island, and his lips were cracked and chapped. His dark eyes were exceedingly clear, but their clarity was not that of intellectuality—it was a gift that the sea bestows upon those who make their livelihood upon it; as a matter of fact, he had made notably bad grades in school. He was still wearing the same clothes he fished in each day—a pair of trousers inherited from his dead father and a cheap jumper.

The boy passed through the already deserted playground of the elementary school and climbed the hill beside the watermill. Mounting the flight of stone steps, he went on behind Yashiro Shrine. Peach blossoms were blooming in the shrine garden, dim and wrapped in twilight. From this point it was not more than a ten-minute climb on up to the lighthouse.

The path to the lighthouse was dangerously steep and winding, so much so that a person unaccustomed to it would surely have lost his footing even in the daytime. But the boy could have closed his eyes, and his feet would still have picked their way unerringly among the rocks and exposed pine roots. Even now when he was deep in his own thoughts, he did not once stumble.

A little while ago, while a few rays of daylight yet remained, the boat on which the boy worked had returned to its home port of Uta-jima. Today, as every day, the boy had gone out fishing on the *Taihei-maru*, a small, engine-powered boat, together with its owner and one other boy. Returning to port, they transferred their catch to the Co-operative's boat and then pulled their own up onto the beach. Then the boy started for home, carrying the halibut he was going to take shortly to the lighthouse. As he came along the beach the twilight was still noisy with the shouts of fishermen pulling their boats up onto the sand.

There was a girl he had never seen before. She leaned resting against a stack of heavy wooden frames lying on the sand, the kind called "abacuses" because of their shape. The fishing-boats were pulled up onto the beach stern-first by means of a winch, and these frames were placed under the keels so they went sliding smoothly over one after another. Apparently the girl had just finished helping with the work of carrying these frames and had paused here to get her breath.

Her forehead was moist with sweat and her cheeks glowed. A cold west wind was blowing briskly, but the girl seemed to enjoy it, turning her work-flushed face into the wind and letting her hair stream out behind her. She was wearing a sleeveless, cotton-padded jacket, women's work-pants gathered at the ankles, and a pair of soiled work-gloves. The healthy color of her skin was no different from that of the other island girls, but there was some-

7

thing refreshing about the cast of her eyes, something serene about her eyebrows. The girl's eyes were turned intently toward the sky over the sea to the west. There a crimson spot of sun was sinking between piles of blackening clouds.

The boy could not remember ever having seen this girl before. There should not have been a single face on Utajima that he could not recognize. At first glance he took her for an outsider. But still, the girl's dress was not that of outsiders. Only in the way she stood apart, gazing at the sea, did she differ from the vivacious island girls.

The boy purposely passed directly in front of the girl. In the same way that children stare at a strange object, he stopped and looked her full in the face.

The girl drew her eyebrows together slightly. But she continued staring fixedly out to sea, never turning her eyes toward the boy.

Finishing his silent scrutiny, he had gone quickly on his way. . . .

At the time he had felt only the vague satisfaction of curiosity gratified, and it was only now, much later, while climbing the path to the lighthouse, that he realized how rude his inspection had been. The thought filled his cheeks with shame.

The boy looked down at the sea between the pine trees along the path. The incoming tide was roaring, and the sea was quite black now before the moon rose. Turning the bend around what was known as Woman's Slope—the ghost of a tall woman was said sometimes to appear here —he caught sight for the first time of the brightly lighted windows of the lighthouse, still high above him. The brightness blinded him for a moment: the village generator had been out of order for a long time and he was accustomed only to the dim light of oil lamps in the village.

The boy often brought fish in this way to the lighthouse, feeling a debt of gratitude toward the lighthouse-keeper. He had flunked his final examinations last year, and it had seemed his graduation would have to be postponed a year. But his mother, on her frequent trips past the lighthouse to gather firewood on the mountain beyond, had struck up an acquaintance with the mistress of the lighthouse, to whom she now appealed. She explained that she simply couldn't support her family any longer if her son's graduation were postponed.

So the lighthouse-keeper's wife spoke to her husband, and he went to see his good friend the school principal. Thanks to this friendly intervention, the boy had finally been able to graduate on schedule.

The boy had become a fisherman as soon as he finished school. And since then he had made it a point to take part of the day's catch to the lighthouse from time to time. He also performed other small errands for them and had become a favorite of both the lighthouse-keeper and his wife.

The residence provided the lighthouse-keeper was just to the side of a flight of concrete steps leading up to the lighthouse itself and had its own small vegetable garden. As the boy approached, he could see the wife's shadow moving about on the glass door of the kitchen. She was evidently preparing supper.

He announced himself by calling from outside and the wife opened the door.

"Oh, it's you, Shinji-san," she said.

The boy held the fish out without a word.

The woman took it from him and called out loudly over her shoulder, this time using the boy's family name:

"Father, Kubo-san has brought us a fish."

From another room the good-natured voice of the light-house-keeper answered familiarly:

"Thank you, thank you. Come on in, Shinji boy."

The boy was still standing hesitantly at the kitchen door. The halibut had already been placed on a white enamelware platter, where it lay faintly gasping, blood oozing from its gills, streaking its smooth white skin.

## 2

Next morning Shinji boarded his master's boat as usual and they set out for the day's fishing. The overcast sky of daybreak was mirrored in a calm sea. It would take about an hour to reach the fishing grounds.

Shinji was wearing a black rubber apron reaching from the breast of his jumper to the tops of his knee-length rubber boots, and a pair of long rubber gloves. Standing in the bow of the boat and gazing ahead to their destination in the Pacific, far ahead under the ashen morning sky, Shinji was remembering the night before, the time between his leaving the lighthouse and going to bed.

Shinji's mother and brother had been awaiting his return in the small room lit by a dim lamp hanging over the cookstove. The brother was only twelve. As for the mother, ever since the last year of the war, when her husband had been killed in a strafing attack, until Shinji had become old enough to go to work, she had supported the family all alone on her earnings as a diving woman.

"Was the lighthouse-keeper pleased?"

"Yes. He said: 'Come in, come in,' and then asked me to have something they called cocoa."

"What was it, this cocoa?"

"Some sort of foreign bean soup is what it seemed like."

The mother knew nothing about cooking. She served their fish either in raw slices—sometimes vinegared—or else simply grilled or boiled—head, tail, bones, and all. And as she never washed the fish properly, they often found their teeth chewing on sand and grit as well as fish.

Shinji waited hopefully during their meal for his mother to say something about the strange girl. But if his mother was not one for complaining, neither was she given to idle gossip.

After supper Shinji and his brother went to the public bath. Here again he hoped to hear something about the girl. As the hour was late, the place was almost empty and the water was dirty. The head of the fishermen's Co-operative and the postmaster were arguing politics as they soaked in the pool, their booming voices echoing pompously off the ceiling. The brothers nodded to them silently and then went to a far corner to dip hot water from the pool.

No matter how Shinji waited and strained his ears, the men simply would not move on from their politics to talk of the girl. Meanwhile his brother had finished bathing with unusual haste and had gone outside.

Shinji followed him out and asked the reason for all his hurry. Hiroshi, the brother, explained that he and his friends had been playing at war today, and that he had made the son of the head of the Co-operative cry by hitting him over the head with his wooden sword.

Shinji always went to sleep easily, but last night he had had the strange experience of lying long awake. Unable to remember a day of sickness in his life, the boy had lain wondering, afraid this might be what people meant by being sick. . . .

That strange unrest was still with him this morning. But the vast ocean stretched away from the prow, where he was standing, and gradually the sight of it filled his body with the energy of familiar, day-to-day toil, and without realizing it he felt at peace again. The boat was shaking mincingly with the vibrations of the engine, and the biting morning wind slapped at the boy's cheeks.

High on the cliff to starboard, the beacon of the lighthouse was already extinguished. Along the shore, under the brownish pine branches of early spring, the pounding breakers of Irako Channel showed vivid white in the cloudy morning landscape. Two submerged reefs in the channel kept the water in a constant churning turmoil; an ocean liner would have had to work its way gingerly through the narrow passage between them, but with the skillful sculling of its master the *Taihei-maru* sailed smoothly through the swirling current. The water in the channel was between eighteen and a hundred fathoms deep, but over the reefs it was only thirteen to twenty fathoms. It was here, from this spot where buoys marked the passage, on out to the Pacific, that the numberless octopus pots were sunk.

Eighty per cent of Uta-jima's yearly catch was in octopus. The octopus season, which began in November, was now about to give way to the squid season, which would begin with the spring equinox. It was the end of the season, the time when the pots were lying in wait for their last chance at what were called the "fleeing octopus" as they moved to the depths of the Pacific to escape the cold waters of the Gulf of Ise.

To master fishermen the exact rise and fall of every inch of the bottom of the shallow waters off the Pacific side of the island were as familiar as their own kitchen gardens. They were always saying: "It's only a blind man that can't see the ocean floor." They knew their direction from their mariner's compass, and by watching the changing outline of the mountains on the far distant capes they could always tell their exact position. Once they had their bearings, they unerringly knew the topography of the ocean floor beneath them.

Countless ropes had been methodically laid out over the floor of the ocean, to each of which were tied more than a hundred pots, and the floats attached to the ropes rolled and tossed with the rise and fall of the tides. In their boat it was the master who knew the art of octopus fishing; all Shinji and the other boy, Ryuji, had to do was lend their strong bodies willingly to the heavy labor involved.

Jukichi Oyama, master fisherman, owner of the *Taihei-maru*, had a face like leather well-tanned by sea winds. The grimy wrinkles on his hands were mixed indistinguishably with old fishing scars, all burned by the sun down into their deepest creases. He was a man who seldom laughed, but was always in calm good spirits, and even the loud voice he used when giving commands on the boat was never raised in anger. While fishing he seldom left his place on the sculling platform at the stern, only occasionally taking one hand off the oar to regulate the engine.

Emerging into the fishing grounds, they found already gathered there the many other fishing-boats, unseen until now, and exchanged morning greetings with them. Upon reaching their own fishing area, Jukichi reduced the speed of the engine and signaled Shinji to attach a belt from the engine to the roller-shaft on the gunwale.

This shaft turned a pulley which extended over the gunwale. One of the ropes to which the octopus pots were tied would be placed over the pulley, and the boat would slowly follow the rope along as the pulley drew one end up from the sea and let the other fall back into the sea. The two boys also would take turns at pulling on the rope, because the water-soaked hemp was often too heavy a load for the pulley alone and also because the rope would slip off unless carefully guided.

A hazy sun was hidden behind the clouds on the horizon. Two or three cormorants were swimming on the sea, their long necks thrust out over the surface of the water. Looking back toward Uta-jima, one could see its southern cliffs shining, dead-white, stained by the droppings of countless flocks of cormorants.

The wind was bitterly cold, but while he pulled the first rope toward the pulley Shinji stared out over the dark-indigo sea and felt boiling up within him energy for the toil that would soon have him sweating. The pulley began to turn and heavy, wet rope came rising from the sea. Through his thin gloves Shinji could feel the thick, icy rope he grasped in his hands. As it passed over the pulley the taut rope threw off a sleet-like spray of salt water.

Soon the octopus pots themselves were rising to the

surface, showing a red-clay color. Ryuji stood waiting at the pulley. If a pot was empty, he would quickly pour the water out of it and, not letting it strike the pulley, again commit it to the care of the rope, now sinking back into the sea.

Shinji stood with his legs spread wide, one foot stretched to the prow, and continued his endless tug-of-war against whatever there was in the sea. One hand-pull by one hand-pull, the rope came up. Shinji was winning. But the sea was not surrendering: one after the other, mockingly, it kept sending the pots up—all empty.

More than twenty pots had already been pulled up at intervals of from seven to ten yards along the rope. Shinji was pulling the rope. Ryuji was emptying water from the pots. Jukichi, keeping a hand on the sculling oar and never once changing his expression, silently watched the boys at their work.

Sweat gradually spread across Shinji's back and began to glisten on his forehead, exposed to the morning wind. His cheeks became flushed. Finally the sun broke through the clouds, casting pale shadows at the feet of the quickly moving boys.

Ryuji was facing away from the sea, in toward the boat. He upended the pot that had just come up, and Jukichi pulled a lever to disengage the pulley. Now for the first time Shinji looked back toward the pulley.

Ryuji poked around inside the pot with a wooden pole. Like a person awakened from a long nap, an octopus oozed its entire body out of the pot and cowered on the deck. Quickly the cover was jerked off a large bamboo creel standing by the engine room—and the first catch of the day went slithering down into it with a dull thud.

. . .

The *Taihei-maru* spent most of the morning octopus fishing. Its meager catch consisted of five octopuses. The wind died and the sun shone gloriously. Passing through the Irako Channel, the *Taihei-maru* sailed back into the Gulf of Ise to do some "drag fishing" on the sly in the prohibited waters there.

To make their drag they tied a number of large hooks and lines on a crossbar, tied it to a stout hawser, and then, putting the boat in motion, dragged this across the floor of the gulf like a rake. After a time they pulled the drag in; with it four flatheads and three soles came flapping up from the water.

Shinji took them off the hooks with his bare hands. The flatheads fell to the blood-smeared deck, their white bellies gleaming. The black, wet bodies of the soles, their little eyes sunk deep in folds of wrinkles, reflected the blue of the sky.

Lunchtime came. Jukichi dressed the flatheads on the engine-room hatch and cut them into slices. They divided the raw slices onto the lids of their aluminum lunchboxes and poured soy sauce over them from a small bottle. Then they took up the boxes, filled with a mixture of boiled rice and barley and, stuffed into one corner, a few slices of pickled radish. The boat they entrusted to the gentle swell.

"Say, what do you think about old Uncle Teru Miyata bringing his girl back?" Jukichi said abruptly.

"I didn't know he had."

"Me neither."

Both boys shook their heads and Jukichi proceeded with his story:

"Uncle Teru had four girls and one boy. Said he had

17

more than enough of girls, so he married three of them off and let the other one be adopted away. Her name was Hatsue and she was adopted into a family of diving women over at Oizaki in Shima. But then, what do you know, that only son of his, Matsu, dies of the lung sickness last year. Being a widower, Uncle Teru starts feeling lonely. So he calls Hatsue back, has her put back in his family register, and decides to adopt a husband into the family for her, to have someone to carry on the name. . . . Hatsue's grown up to be a real beauty. There'll be a lot of youngsters wanting to marry her. . . . How about you two—hey?"

Shinji and Ryuji looked at each other and laughed. Each could guess that the other was blushing, but they were too tanned by the sun for the red to show.

Talk of this girl and the image of the girl he had seen on the beach yesterday immediately took fast hold of each other in Shinji's mind. At the same instant he recalled, with a sinking heart, his own poor condition in life. The recollection made the girl whom he had stared at so closely only the day before seem very, very far away from him now. Because now he knew that her father was Terukichi Miyata, the wealthy owner of two coasting freighters chartered to Yamagawa Transport—the hundred-and-eighty-five-ton *Utajima-maru* and the ninety-five-ton *Harukaze-maru*—and a noted crosspatch, whose white hair would wave like lion whiskers in anger.

Shinji had always been very level-headed. He had realized that he was still only eighteen and that it was too soon to be thinking about women. Unlike the environment of city youths, always exploding with thrills, Utajima had not a single pin-ball parlor, not a single bar, not a single waitress. And this boy's simple daydream was only to own his own engine-powered boat some day and go into the coastal-shipping business with his younger brother.

Surrounded though he was by the vast ocean, Shinji did not especially burn with impossible dreams of great adventure across the seas. His fisherman's conception of the sea was close to that of the farmer for his land. The sea was the place where he earned his living, a rippling field where, instead of waving heads of rice or wheat, the white and formless harvest of waves was forever swaying above the unrelieved blueness of a sensitive and yielding soil.

Even so, when that day's fishing was almost done, the sight of a white freighter sailing against the evening clouds on the horizon filled the boy's heart with strange emotions. From far away the world came pressing in upon him with a hugeness he had never before apprehended. The realization of this unknown world came to him like distant thunder, now pealing from afar, now dying away to nothingness.

A small starfish had dried to the deck in the prow. The boy sat there in the prow, with a coarse white towel tied round his head. He turned his eyes away from the evening clouds and shook his head slightly.

# 3

THAT NIGHT Shinji attended the regular meeting of the Young Men's Association. This was the name now applied to what in ancient times was called the "sleeping house," then a dormitory system for the young, unmarried men of the island. Even now many young men preferred to sleep in the Association's drab hut on the beach rather than in their own homes. There the youths hotly debated such matters as schooling and health; the ways of salvaging sunken ships and making rescues at sea; and the Lion and Lantern Festival dances, functions belonging to the young men of the village since ancient days. Thus they felt themselves part of the communal life and found pleasure in that agreeable weight that comes from shouldering the burdens and duties of full-grown men.

A wind was blowing from the sea, rattling the closed

night-shutters and making the lamp sway back and forth, now dim, now suddenly bright. From outside, the night sea came pressing very near them, and the roar of the tide was constantly revealing the unrest and might of nature as the shadows of the lamp moved over the cheerful faces of the young men.

When Shinji entered the hut one boy was kneeling on all fours under the lamp, having his hair cut by a friend with a pair of slightly rusty hair clippers. Shinji smiled and sat down on the floor against the wall, clasping his knees. He remained silent as usual, listening to what the others were saying.

The youths were bragging to each other of the day's fishing, laughing loudly and heaping each other unstintingly with insults. One boy, who was a great reader, was earnestly reading one of the out-of-date magazines with which the hut was supplied. Another was engrossed, with no less enthusiasm, in a comic book; holding the pages open with fingers whose knuckles were gnarled beyond his years, he would study some pages for two or three minutes at a time before finally understanding the point and breaking into a loud guffaw.

Here, for the second time, Shinji heard talk of the new girl. He caught a snatch of a sentence spoken by a snaggle-toothed boy who opened a big mouth to laugh and then said:

"That Hatsue, she's—"

The rest of the sentence was lost to Shinji in a sudden commotion from another part of the room, mixed with answering laughter from the group around the snaggle-toothed boy.

Shinji was not at all given to brooding about things, but this one name, like a tantalizing puzzle, kept harassing his thoughts. At the mere sound of the name his cheeks flushed and his heart pounded. It was a strange feeling to sit there motionless and feel within himself these physical changes that, until now, he had experienced only during heavy labor.

He put the palm of his hand against his cheek to feel it. The hot flesh felt like that of some complete stranger. It was a blow to his pride to realize the existence of things within himself that he had never so much as suspected, and rising anger made his cheeks even more flaming hot.

The young men were awaiting the arrival of their president, Yasuo Kawamoto. Although only nineteen, Yasuo was the son of a leading family in the village and possessed the power to make others follow him. Young as he was, he already knew the secret of giving himself importance, and he always came late to their meetings.

Opening the door with a bang, Yasuo now entered the room. He was quite fat and had inherited a red complexion from his tippling father. His face was naïve enough in appearance, but there was a crafty look about his thin eyebrows. He spoke glibly, without any trace of the local dialect:

"Sorry to be late. . . . Well, then, let's not waste time. There're definite plans to be made for next month's projects."

So saying, he sat down at the desk and opened a notebook. They could all see that he was in a great hurry about something.

"As decided at the last meeting, there's the business of ·—er—holding a meeting of the Respect for Old Age Association, and also hauling stones for road repairs. Then there's the matter of cleaning the sewers to get rid of the rats—it's a request of the Village Assembly. We'll do this as usual—er—on a stormy day when the boats can't go out. Fortunately, rat-catching can be done in any weather, and I don't believe the police will get after us even if we kill a few rats outside the sewers."

There was general laughter and shouts of "You tell 'em! You tell 'em!"

Next, proposals were made to ask the school doctor to give them a talk on hygiene, and to hold an oratorical contest. But the old-style, lunar-calendar New Year was just over, and the youths were so fed up with gatherings that they were lukewarm to both proposals.

So they turned themselves into a committee of the whole and sat in critical judgment on the merits of their mimeographed bulletin, *The Orphan Island*. Something called a quatrain by Verlaine had been quoted at the end of an essay in the last issue by the boy who liked books so much, and this now became the universal target for their jibes:

> *I know not why*
> *My mournful soul*
> *Flies the sea, fitfully, fitfully,*
> *On restless, frantic pinions . . .*

"What do you mean by that 'fitfully, fitfully'?"

"'Fitfully, fitfully' means 'fitfully, fitfully'—that's what!"

"Maybe it's a mistake for 'flitfully, flitfully.'"

"That's it! If you'd said 'it flies flitfully, flitfully'—then that would've made some sense."

"Who's this Verlaine fellow anyhow?"

"One of the most famous French poets—that's who!"

23

"And what do you know about French poets, hey? You probably got it all out of some popular song somewhere."

Thus the meeting had ended as usual in a give-and-take of insults.

Wondering why Yasuo, the president, had been in such a hurry to leave, Shinji stopped one of his friends and asked him.

"Don't you know?" the friend replied. "He's invited to the party Uncle Teru Miyata's giving to celebrate his daughter's homecoming."

Normally Shinji would have walked home with the others as they talked and laughed, but now, hearing of the party to which in no case would he have been invited, he soon slipped away and walked alone along the beach toward the stone steps leading to Yashiro Shrine.

Looking up at the village houses, built one above the other on a steep rise, he picked out the lights shining from the Miyata house. All the lights in the village came from the same oil lamps, but these looked somehow different, more sparkling. Even if he could not see the actual scene of the banquet, he could clearly imagine how the sensitive flame of the lamps there must be throwing flickering shadows from the girl's tranquil eyebrows and long lashes down onto her cheeks.

Reaching the bottom of the stone steps, Shinji looked up the flight of stairs, dappled with shadows of pine branches. He began to climb, his wooden clogs making a dry, clicking sound. There was not a soul to be seen around the shrine, and the light in the priest's house was out.

Even though he had just bounded up two hundred steps, Shinji's thick chest was not laboring in the least when he reached the shrine. He stopped before it, filled with a feeling of reverence.

He tossed a ten-yen coin into the offertory chest. Thinking a moment, he tossed in ten yen more. The sound of his clapped hands, calling the god's attention, sounded through the shrine garden, and Shinji prayed in his heart:

"God, let the seas be calm, the fish plentiful, and our village more and more prosperous. I am still young, but in time let me become a fisherman among fishermen. Let me have much knowledge in the ways of the sea, in the ways of fish, in the ways of boats, in the ways of the weather . . . in everything. Let me be a man with surpassing skill in everything. . . . Please protect my gentle mother and my brother, who is still a child. When my mother enters the sea in the diving season, please protect her body somehow from all the many dangers. . . . Then there's a different sort of request I'd like to make. . . . Some day let even such a person as me be granted a good-natured, beautiful bride . . . say someone like Terukichi Miyata's returned daughter. . . ."

The wind came blowing, and the pine branches set up a clamor. It was a gust of wind that raised solemn echoes even in the dark interior of the shrine. Perhaps it was the sea-god, accepting the boy's prayer.

Shinji looked up at the star-filled sky and breathed deeply. Then he thought:

"But mightn't the gods punish me for such a selfish prayer?"

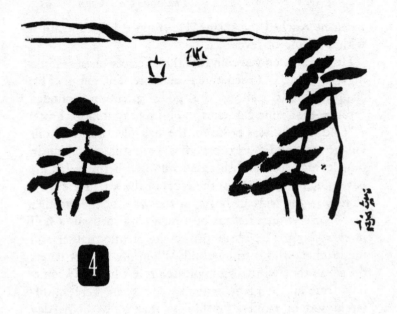

## 4

IT WAS some four or five days later and the wind was blowing a gale. The waves were breaking high across the breakwater of Uta-jima's harbor. The sea, far and wide, was choppy with whitecaps.

The skies were clear, but because of the high wind not a single fishing-boat had gone out.

Shinji's mother had asked a favor of him. The women of the village gathered firewood on the mountain and left it stored at the top in what had formerly been a military observation tower. His mother had marked hers with a red rag. Since he had finished by noon with the Young Men's Association's work of carrying stones for the road building, she asked him to bring her gatherings down from the mountain for her.

.　.　.

Shinji shouldered the wooden frame on which brush-wood was carried, and set out. The path led up past the lighthouse. As he rounded Woman's Slope the wind died as completely as though it had been a trick.

The residence of the lighthouse-keeper was as quiet as though in a deep noonday sleep. He could see the back of a watchman seated at the desk in the watchhouse. A radio was blaring music.

Climbing the pine-grove slope behind the lighthouse, Shinji began to sweat.

The mountain was utterly still. Not a single human form was to be seen; there was not even so much as a stray dog prowling about. In fact, because of a taboo of the island's guardian deity, there was not a single stray dog on the entire island, let alone a pet dog. And as the island was all uphill and land was scarce, neither were there any horses or cows for draft animals. The only domestic animals were the cats that came trailing the tips of their tails through the jagged shadows thrown in sharp relief in the lanes leading always downward in cobbled steps between the rows of village houses.

The boy climbed to the top of the mountain. This was the highest point on Uta-jima. But it was so overgrown with *sakaki* and silverberry bushes and tall weeds that there was no view. There was nothing but the sound of the sea roaring up through the vegetation. The path leading down the other side to the south had been practically taken over by bushes and weeds, and one had to make quite a detour to reach the observation tower.

Presently, beyond a sand-floored pine thicket, the three-story, reinforced-concrete tower came into view. The white ruins looked uncanny in the deserted, silent scene.

In former days soldiers had stood on the second-floor

balcony, binoculars to their eyes, and checked the aim of the guns that were fired for target practice from Mt. Konaka on the far side of Irako Cape. Officers had called out from inside the tower to know where the shells were hitting, and the soldiers had called back the ranges. This way of things had continued until mid-war, and the soldiers had always blamed a phantom badger for any provisions that were mysteriously short.

The boy peeped into the ground floor of the tower. There was a mountain of dried pine needles and twigs tied into bundles. This floor had evidently been used as a storehouse, and its windows were quite small; there were even some with their glass panes still unbroken. The boy entered and, by the faint light of the windows, soon found his mother's mark—red rags tied to several bundles, the name "Tomi Kubo" written on them in childish characters.

Taking the frame off his back, Shinji tied the bundles of dried needles and twigs to it. He had not visited the tower for a long time and now felt reluctant to depart so soon. Leaving the load lying where it was, he was about to start up the concrete steps.

Just then there was a faint sound from overhead as though of stone and wood striking together. The boy listened intently. The sound ceased. It must have been his imagination.

He went on up the stairs, and there on the second floor of the ruins was the sea, framed desolately in wide windows which lacked both glass and casings. Even the iron railing of the balcony was gone. Traces of the soldiers' chalk scribblings could still be seen on the gray walls.

Shinji continued climbing. He paused to look at the

broken flagpole out a third-story window—and this time he was certain he heard the sound of someone's sobbing. He gave a start and ran lightly on up to the roof on sneaker-clad feet.

The one who was really startled was the girl on the roof, having a boy suddenly appear before her out of nowhere, without so much as a footfall. She was wearing wooden clogs and was weeping, but now she ceased her sobbing and stood petrified with fear. It was Hatsue.

As for the boy, he had never dreamed of such a fortunate meeting and could not believe his eyes.

So the two of them simply stood there, startled, like animals that come suddenly face to face in the forest, looking into each other's eyes, their emotions wavering between caution and curiosity.

Finally Shinji spoke:

"You're Hatsue-san, aren't you?"

Hatsue nodded involuntarily and then looked surprised at his knowing her name. But something about the black, serious eyes of this boy who was making such an effort to put up a bold front seemed to remind her of a young face that had gazed at her fixedly on the beach the other day.

"It was you crying, wasn't it?"

"Yes, it was me."

"Why were you crying?" Shinji sounded like a policeman.

Her reply came with unexpected promptness. The mistress of the lighthouse gave lessons in etiquette and homemaking for the girls of the village who were interested, and today Hatsue was going to attend for the first time. But, coming too early, she had decided to climb the mountain behind the lighthouse and had lost her way.

Just then the shadow of a bird swept over their heads. It was a peregrine. Shinji took this for a lucky sign. Thereupon his tangled tongue came unloose and, recovering his usual air of manliness, he told her that he passed the lighthouse on his way home and would go that far with her.

Hatsue smiled, making not the slightest effort to wipe away the tears that had flowed down her cheeks. It was as though the sun had come shining through rain. She was wearing a red sweater, blue-serge slacks, and red-velvet socks—the split-toed kind worn with clogs.

Hatsue leaned over the concrete parapet at the edge of the roof and looked down at the sea.

"What's this building?" she asked.

Shinji too went to the parapet, but at a little distance from the girl.

"It used to be a target-observation tower," he answered. "They watched from here to see where the cannon shells landed."

Here on the south side of the island, screened by the mountain, there was no wind. The sunlit expanse of the Pacific stretched away beneath their eyes. The pine-clad cliff dropped abruptly to the sea, its jutting rocks stained white with cormorant droppings, and the water near the base of the cliff was black-brown from the seaweed growing on the ocean floor.

Shinji pointed to a tall rock just offshore where the surging waves were striking, sending up clouds of spray.

"That's called Black Isle," he explained. "It's where Policeman Suzuki was fishing when the waves washed him away and drowned him."

Shinji was thoroughly happy. But the time was drawing near when Hatsue was due at the lighthouse. Straightening up from the concrete parapet, she turned toward Shinji.

"I'll be going now," she said.

Shinji made no answer and a surprised look came over his face. He had caught sight of a black streak that ran straight across the front of her red sweater.

Hatsue followed his gaze and saw the dirty smudge, just in the spot where she had been leaning her breast against the concrete parapet. Bending her head, she started slapping her breast with her open hands. Beneath her sweater, which all but seemed to be concealing some firm supports, two gently swelling mounds were set to trembling ever so slightly by the brisk brushing of her hands.

Shinji stared in wonder. Struck by her hands, the breasts seemed more like two small, playful animals. The boy was deeply stirred by the resilient softness of their movement.

The streak of dirt was finally brushed out.

Shinji went first down the concrete steps and Hatsue followed, her clogs making very clear, light sounds which echoed from the four walls of the ruins. But the sounds behind Shinji's back came to a stop as they were reaching the first floor.

Shinji looked back. The girl was standing there, laughing.

"What is it?" he asked.

"I'm dark too, but you—you're practically *black*."

"What?"

"You've *really* been burnt by the sun, you have."

The boy laughed in meaningless reply and went on

down the stairs. They were just about to leave the tower when he stopped abruptly and ran back inside. He had almost forgotten his mother's bundles.

On the way back toward the lighthouse Shinji walked in front, carrying the mountain of pine needles on his back. As they walked along, the girl asked him his name and now, for the first time, he introduced himself. But he went on hurriedly to ask that she not mention his name to anyone or say anything about having met him here: Shinji well knew how sharp the villagers' tongues could be. Hatsue promised not to tell. Thus their well-founded fear of the village's love of gossip changed what was but an innocent meeting into a thing of secrecy between the two of them.

Shinji walked on in silence, having no idea how they could meet again, and soon they reached the spot from which they could look down upon the lighthouse. He pointed out the short cut leading down to the rear of the lighthouse-keeper's residence and told her good-by. Then, purposely, he took the roundabout way on down to the village.

# 5

UNTIL NOW the boy had been leading a peaceful, contented existence, poor though he was, but from this time on he became tormented with unrest and lost in thought, falling prey to the feeling that there was nothing about him that could possibly appeal to Hatsue. He was so healthy that he had never had any sickness other than the measles. He could swim the circumference of Uta-jima as many as five times without stopping. And he was sure he would have to yield to no one in any test of physical strength. But he could not believe that any of these qualities could possibly touch Hatsue's heart.

Another opportunity to meet Hatsue simply would not come. Whenever he returned from fishing he always looked all along the beach for her, but on the few occasions when he caught sight of her she was busy working and there was no chance to speak.

There was no such thing as that time when she had been alone, leaning against the "abacuses" and staring out to sea. Moreover, whenever the boy resolved that he was sick of it all and that he would put Hatsue completely out of his mind, on that very day he was sure to catch sight of her among the bustling crowd that gathered on the beach when the boats came in.

City youths learn the ways of love early from novels, movies, and the like, but on Uta-jima there were practically no models to follow. Thus, no matter how he wondered about it, Shinji had not the slightest idea what he should have done during those precious minutes between the observation tower and the lighthouse when he had been alone with her. He was left with nothing but a keen sense of regret, a feeling that there was something he had utterly failed to do.

It was the monthly commemoration of the day of his father's death, and the whole family was going to visit the grave, as they did every month. Not to interfere with Shinji's work, they had chosen a time before the boats set out, and before his brother's school.

Shinji and his brother came out of the house with their mother, who was carrying incense sticks and grave flowers. They left the house standing open: there was no such thing as theft on the island.

The graveyard was located some distance from the village, on a low cliff above the beach. At high tide the sea came right up to the foot of the cliff. The uneven slope was covered with gravestones, some of them tilting on the soft sand foundation.

Dawn had not yet broken. The sky was just beginning to become light in the direction of the lighthouse, but the village and its harbor, which faced northwest, still remained in night.

Shinji walked in front carrying a paper lantern. Hiroshi, his brother, was still rubbing the sleep out of his eyes when he pulled on his mother's sleeve and said:

"Can I have four rice dumplings in my lunch today? Can I, huh?"

"Such foolishness! *Two* you'll get. Three'd more than give you the bellyache."

"Please! I want *four!*"

The rice dumplings they made on the island to celebrate the Day of the Monkey, or on death-memorial days, were almost as large as the small pillows they slept on.

In the graveyard a cold morning breeze was blowing fitfully. The surface of the sea in the lee of the island was black, but the offing was stained with dawn. The mountains enclosing the Gulf of Ise could be seen clearly. In the pale light of daybreak the gravestones looked like so many white sails of boats anchored in a busy harbor. They were sails that would never again be filled with wind, sails that, too long unused and heavily drooping, had been turned into stone just as they were. The boats' anchors had been thrust so deeply into the dark earth that they could never again be raised.

Reaching their father's grave, their mother arranged the flowers she had brought and, after striking many matches only to have them blown out by the wind, finally succeeded in lighting the incense. Then she had her sons bow before the grave, while she herself bowed behind them, weeping.

.   .   .

In their village there was a saying: "Never have aboard one woman or one priest." The boat on which Shinji's father died had broken this taboo. An old woman had died on the island toward the end of the war, and the Co-operative's boat had set out to take her body to Toshi-jima for the autopsy.

When the boat was about three miles out from Uta-jima it was sighted by a plane from an aircraft carrier. The boat's regular engineer was not aboard and his substitute was unaccustomed to the engine. It was the black smoke from his sluggish engine that had given the plane its target.

The plane dropped a bomb on the boat and then strafed it with machine-gun fire. The boat's funnel was split open, and Shinji's father had his head torn apart down to his ears. Another man too was killed instantly, hit in the eye. One was hit in the back by a bullet, which entered his lungs. One was hit in the legs. And one who had a buttock shot away died shortly after of the bleeding.

Both the deck and the bilge became a lake of blood. The fuel tank was hit and kerosene spread on top of the blood. Some hesitated to fling themselves prone in this mess and were hit in the hips. Four persons saved themselves by taking shelter in the icebox in the forward cabin. In his panic, one man squeezed himself through the porthole behind the bridge, but when he tried to repeat the feat back in port he found that, no matter how he tried, he could not wriggle through that tiny opening a second time.

Thus, of eleven persons, three were killed and a number wounded. But the corpse of the old woman, stretched out on the deck under a rush mat, was not so much as touched by a single bullet. . . .

.    .    .

"The old man was really something fierce when fishing for sand launce," Shinji said reminiscently to his mother. "He'd beat me every day. Really, there wasn't time for the welts to go down before he'd raise more."

Sand launce were found in the Yohiro Shallows, and catching them required unusual skill. A flexible bamboo pole with feathers on the tip was used to imitate a sea-bird pursuing a fish under the water, and the operation called for split-second timing.

"Well, I guess so," said his mother. "Sand-launce fishing is real man's work even for a fisherman."

Hiroshi took no interest in the talk between his mother and brother but was dreaming of the school excursion that was to take place in only ten days more. Shinji had been too poor to go on school excursions when he was Hiroshi's age, so he had been saving money out of his own wages for Hiroshi's travel expenses.

When they had finished paying their homage at the graveside, Shinji went on alone directly to the beach to help with the preparations for sailing. It was agreed that his mother would return home and bring him his lunch before the boats put out.

As he hurried toward the *Taihei-maru* along the busy beach, someone's voice from out of the throng came to him on the wind and struck his ears:

"They say Yasuo Kawamoto's to marry Hatsue."

At the sound of those words Shinji's spirits became pitch-black.

Again the *Taihei-maru* spent the day octopus fishing. During the eleven hours they were out in the boat Shinji threw his whole soul into the fishing and scarcely once opened his mouth. But as he usually had very little to say, his silence was not particularly noticeable.

Returning to harbor, they tied up as usual to the Co-operative's boat and unloaded their octopuses. Then the other fish were sold through a middleman and transferred to the "buyer ship" belonging to a private wholesale fish dealer. The giltheads were flapping about inside the metal baskets used for weighing fish, flashing in the light of the setting sun.

It was the day out of every ten when the fishermen were paid, so Shinji and Ryuji went along with the master to the office of the Co-operative. Their catch for the ten-day period had been over three hundred and thirty pounds and they cleared 27,997 yen after deducting the Co-operative's sales commission, the ten per cent savings deposit, and maintenance costs. Shinji received four thousand yen from the master as his share. It had been a good take considering that the height of the fishing season was already past.

Licking his fingers, the boy carefully counted the bills in his big, rough hands. Then he returned them to the envelope with his name on it and put it deep in the bottom of the inner pocket of his jumper. With a bow toward the master, he left the office. The master had drawn up to the brazier with the head of the Co-operative and was proudly exhibiting a cigarette holder he had carved himself out of a piece of coral.

The boy had intended to go straight home, but somehow his feet took him of their own accord back to the darkening beach.

The last boat was just being pulled up onto the sand. There were only a few men to turn the winch and to help it along by pulling on the rope, so the women, who usually only placed the "abacus" frames under the keel, were pushing from behind. It was obvious that no headway was being made. The beach was growing dark and no trace was to be seen of the grammar-school boys who usually came out to help. Shinji decided to lend a hand.

Just at that moment one of the women pushing the boat raised her head and looked in Shinji's direction. It was Hatsue. He had no wish to see the face of this girl who had put him in such a black mood all day. But his feet carried him on to the boat. Her face was glowing in the semidarkness; he could see her forehead moist with sweat, her rosy cheeks, her dark, flashing eyes fixed again steadily in the direction the boat was being pushed.

Without a word, Shinji took hold of the rope. The men at the winch called out:

"Much obliged."

Shinji's arms were powerful. In an instant the boat was sliding up over the sand, and the women were running helter-skelter after it with their "abacus" frames.

Once the boat was beached, Shinji turned and walked off toward home, not once looking back. He wanted terribly to turn around, but smothered the impulse.

Opening the sliding door of his house, under the dim lamp Shinji saw the familiar expanse of straw mats, turned reddish-brown with age and use. His brother was lying on his stomach reading, holding a textbook out under the light. His mother was busy at the cookstove. Without taking off his rubber boots, Shinji lay back face up, the upper half of his body on the straw mats and his feet still in the tiny entry.

"Welcome back," said his mother.

Shinji liked to hand his pay envelope to his mother without saying anything. And, being a mother, she understood and always pretended to have forgotten that this was the tenth day, payday. She knew how much her son liked to see her look surprised.

Shinji ran his hand into the inner pocket of his jumper. The money was not there! He searched the pocket on the other side. He searched his trouser pockets. He even ran his hands down inside his trousers.

Surely he must have dropped it on the beach. Without a word, he ran out of the house.

Shortly after Shinji had left, someone came calling in front of the house. Shinji's mother went to the entry and found a young girl standing in the darkness of the alleyway.

"Shinji-san—is he at home?"

"He came home just a bit ago, but then he went out again."

"I found this on the beach. And since Shinji-san's name was written on it . . ."

"Well, now that's truly kind of you. Shinji must have gone to look for it."

"Shall I go tell him?"

"Oh, would you? Much obliged, much obliged."

The beach was now completely dark. The meager lights of Toshi-jima and Sugashi-jima were glinting from across the sea. Fast asleep in the starlight, many fishing-boats were lined up, facing domineeringly out to sea.

Hatsue caught a glimpse of Shinji's shadow. But at that instant he disappeared behind a boat. He was stooping over, searching the sand, and apparently had not seen Hatsue. She came upon him face to face in the shadow of a boat, standing stock-still, in a rage.

Hatsue told him what had happened and that she had come to tell him his money was already safely in his mother's hands. She went on to explain that she had had to ask two or three people the way to Shinji's house, but had always satisfied their curiosity by showing them the envelope she had found, with Shinji's name on it.

The boy gave a sigh of relief. He smiled, his white teeth flashing handsomely in the darkness. The girl had come in a hurry and her breasts were rising and falling rapidly. Shinji was reminded of opulent dark-blue waves on the open sea. All the day's torment disappeared, and his spirits revived within him.

"I hear you're going to marry Yasuo Kawamoto. Is it true?" The words rushed out of the boy's mouth.

The girl burst out laughing. Her laughter gradually increased until she was choking with it.

Shinji wanted to stop her but did not know how. He put his hand on her shoulder.

His touch was light, but Hatsue dropped to the sand, still laughing.

"What's the matter? What's the matter?" Shinji squatted down beside her and shook her by the shoulders.

At last the girl's laughter abated and she looked seriously into the boy's face. Then she broke into laughter again.

Shinji stuck out his face toward hers and asked:

"Is it true?"

"Silly! It's a big lie."

"But that's what they're saying all right."

41

"It's a big lie."

The two had clasped their knees and were sitting in the shadow of the boat.

"Oh, I hurt! I've laughed so much that I hurt—right here," the girl said, putting her hand over her breast.

The stripes of her faded work-clothes were moving and shifting where they crossed her breasts.

"This is where it hurts," Hatsue said again.

"Are you all right?" And without thinking Shinji put his own hand on the spot.

"When you press it, it feels a little better," the girl said.

And suddenly Shinji's breast too was moving fast.

Their cheeks came so close they were almost touching. They could plainly smell each other—it was a fragrance like that of salt water. They could feel each other's warmth.

Their dry, chapped lips touched. There was a slight taste of salt.

"It's like seaweed," Shinji thought.

Then the moment was past. The boy moved away and stood up, propelled by a feeling of guilt at this first experience in his life.

"Tomorrow I'm going to take some fish to the lighthouse-keeper's place when I come back from fishing." Still looking out to sea, Shinji had now recovered his dignity and could make this declaration in a manly voice.

"I'm going there too tomorrow afternoon," the girl replied, likewise looking out to sea.

With that, the two parted and went walking away on opposite sides of the row of boats. Shinji was starting for home, but he noticed that the girl had not appeared from behind the boats. Just then he saw her shadow cast on the sand from behind the last boat and knew she was hiding there.

"Your shadow's giving you away," he called out.

Suddenly the figure of a girl dressed in wide-striped work-clothes came darting out, like some wild animal, and went running at full speed across the beach, never looking back.

**6**

Returning from fishing the next day, Shinji set out for the lighthouse carrying two scorpion-fish, each about five or six inches long, strung by the gills on a straw rope. He had already climbed to the rear of Yashiro Shrine when he remembered that he had not yet offered a prayer of thanks to the god for having showered him with blessings so quickly. He went back to the front of the shrine and prayed devoutly.

His prayer finished, Shinji gazed out over the Gulf of Ise, already shining in the moonlight, and breathed deeply. Clouds were floating above the horizon, looking like ancient gods.

The boy felt a consummate accord between himself

44

and this opulence of nature that surrounded him. He inhaled deeply, and it was as though a part of the unseen something that constitutes nature had permeated the core of his being. He heard the sound of the waves striking the shore, and it was as though the surging of his young blood was keeping time with the movement of the sea's great tides. It was doubtless because nature itself satisfied his need that Shinji felt no particular lack of music in his everyday life.

Shinji lifted the scorpion-fish to the level of his eyes and stuck out his tongue at their ugly, thorny faces. The fish were definitely alive, but they made not the slightest movement. So Shinji poked one in the jaw and watched it flop about in the air.

Thus the boy was loitering along the way, loath to have the happy meeting take place too quickly.

Both the lighthouse keeper and his wife had taken Hatsue, the newcomer, to their warm hearts. Just when she was so silent that they were thinking maybe she was not so attractive after all, suddenly she would break into her lovely, girlish laughter; and if she sometimes seemed lost in the clouds, she was also most considerate. For instance, at the end of an etiquette lesson Hatsue would immediately begin clearing away the cups they had drunk their tea in —a thoughtful action that never would have occurred to the other girls—and while she was at it she would go on to wash any other dirty dishes she might find in the kitchen.

The couple at the lighthouse had one child, a daughter, who was attending the university in Tokyo. She only came home during vacations and, in her absence, they regarded these village girls who came so often to the house as their own children. They took a deep interest in the girls' futures, and when good fortune came to one of them they were as pleased as though the girl had been their own child.

The lighthouse-keeper, who had been in this service for thirty years, was feared by the village children because of his stern look and the tremendous voice with which he stormed at the young scamps who stole in to explore the lighthouse; but at heart he was actually a gentle person. Solitude had divested him of any feeling that men could have base motives. At a lighthouse there can be no greater treat than to have visitors. Surely no one would go the great distance to call at an isolated lighthouse with hidden ill-will, or at least any such feelings would surely vanish from his heart in the face of the unreserved hospitality he was certain to receive. Actually, it was just as the lighthouse-keeper so often said: "Bad intentions cannot travel as far as good."

The mistress too was truly a good person, and also very well read. Not only had she once been a teacher in a rural girls' school, but her many years of living in lighthouses had fostered her love of reading even more, until she now possessed an almost encyclopedic knowledge about everything. If she knew that La Scala Opera House was in Milan, she also knew that such-and-such a Tokyo film star had recently sprained her right ankle at such-and-such a place. She would argue her husband into a corner, and then, as if to make amends, put her whole soul into darning his socks or fixing his supper. When visitors came she would chatter away incessantly. The villagers listened spellbound to the mistress's eloquence, some of them comparing her unfavorably with their own taciturn women and feeling a meddlesome sort of sympathy for the lighthouse-keeper. But he himself had great respect for his wife's learning.

The living-quarters provided for the lighthouse-keeper was a one-story house of three rooms. Everything about it was kept as neat and polished as the lighthouse itself. A steamship-company calendar hung on the wall, and the ashes in the sunken hearth of the sitting-room were always neatly shaped up around the charcoal. Even in their daughter's absence, her desk stood in one corner of the parlor, its polished surface reflecting the blue glass of an empty pen-tray and decorated with a French doll. Behind the house there was a caldron-style bath heated by gas made from the dregs of the oil used to lubricate the beacon light. Unlike conditions in the squalid houses of the fishermen, here even the indigo pattern of the new-washed hand towel hanging by the basin at the toilet-room door was always bright and clean.

The lighthouse-keeper spent the greater part of each day beside the sunken hearth, smoking cheap New Life cigarettes, economically cutting them into short lengths and fitting them into a long, slender brass pipe. The lighthouse was dead during the daytime, with only one of the young assistants in the watchhouse to report ship movements.

Toward evening that day, even though no etiquette lesson was scheduled, Hatsue came visiting, bringing a door-gift of some sea-cucumbers wrapped in newspaper. Beneath her blue-serge skirt she was wearing long flesh-colored stockings, and over them red socks. Her sweater was her usual scarlet one.

Hatsue had no sooner entered the house than the mistress began giving advice, not mincing her words:

"When you wear a blue skirt, Hatsue-san, you ought to wear black hose. I know you have some because you were wearing them only the other day."

"Well . . ." Blushing slightly, Hatsue sat down beside the hearth.

At the regular lessons of etiquette and home-making the girls sat listening fairly intently and the mistress spoke in a lecturing tone of voice, but now, seated by the hearth with Hatsue, she began talking in a free and easy way. As her visitor was a young girl, she talked first in a general sort of way about love, and finally got around to asking such direct questions as "Isn't there someone you like very much?" At times, when the lighthouse-keeper saw the girl become rattled, he would ask a teasing question of his own.

When it began to grow late they asked Hatsue several times if she didn't have to get home for supper and if her father wouldn't be waiting for her. It was Hatsue who finally made the suggestion that she help prepare their supper.

Until now Hatsue had simply sat there blushing furiously and looking down at the floor, not so much as touching the refreshments put before her. But, once in the kitchen, she quickly recovered her good spirits. Then, while slicing the sea-cucumbers, she began singing the traditional Ise chorus used on the island for accompanying the Lantern Festival dancing; she had learned it from her aunt the day before:

*Tall chests, long chests, traveling chests—*
*Since your dower is so great, my daughter,*
*You must never think of coming back.*

*But oh, my mother, you ask too much:*
*When the east is cloudy, they say the wind will blow;*
*When the west is cloudy, they say the rain will fall;*
*And when a fair wind changes—*
*Yoi! Sora!—*
*Even the largest ship returns to port.*

"Oh, have you already learned that song, Hatsue-san?" the mistress said. "Here it's already three years since we came here and I don't know it all even yet."

"Well, but it's almost the same as the one we sang at Oizaki," Hatsue answered.

Just then there was the sound of footsteps outside, and from the darkness someone called:

"Good evening."

"That must be Shinji-san," the mistress said, sticking her head out the kitchen door. Then:

"Well, well! More nice fish. Thanks. . . . Father, Kubo-san's brought us more fish."

"Thanks again, thanks again," the lighthouse-keeper called from the hearth. "Come on in, Shinji boy, come on in."

During this confusion of welcome and thanks Shinji and Hatsue exchanged glances. Shinji smiled. Hatsue smiled too. But the mistress happened to turn around suddenly and intercept their smiles.

"Oh, you two already know each other, do you? H'm, it's a small place, this village. But that makes it all the better, so do come on in, Shinji-san— Oh, and by the way, we had a letter from Chiyoko in Tokyo. She particularly asked about Shinji-san. I don't guess there's much doubt about who Chiyoko likes, is there? She'll be coming home soon for spring vacation, so be sure and come to see her."

Shinji had been just on the point of coming into the house for a minute, but these words seemed to wrench his nose. Hatsue turned back to the sink and did not look around again. The boy retreated back into the dusk. They called him several times, but he would not come back. He made his bow from a distance and then took to his heels.

"That Shinji-san—he's really the bashful one, isn't he, Father?" the mistress said, laughing.

The lone sound of her laughter echoed through the house. Neither the lighthouse-keeper nor Hatsue even smiled.

Shinji waited for Hatsue where the path curved around Woman's Slope.

At that point the dusk surrounding the lighthouse gave way to the last faint light that still remained of the sunset. Even though the shadows of the pine trees had become doubly dark, the sea below them was brimming with a last afterglow. All through the day the first easterly winds of spring had been blowing in off the sea, and even now that night was falling the wind did not feel cold on the skin.

As Shinji rounded Woman's Slope even that small wind died away, and there was nothing left in the dusk but calm shafts of radiance pouring down between the clouds.

Looking down, he saw the small promontory that jutted out into the sea to form the far side of Uta-jima's harbor. From time to time its tip was shrugging its rocky shoulders swaggeringly, rending asunder the foaming waves. The vicinity of the promontory was especially bright. Standing on the promontory's peak there was a lone red-pine, its trunk bathed in the afterglow and vividly clear to the boy's keen eyes. Suddenly the trunk lost the last beam of light. The clouds overhead turned black and the stars began to glitter above Mt. Higashi.

Shinji laid his ear against a jutting rock and heard the sound of short, quick footsteps approaching along the flagstone path that led down from the stone steps at the entrance to the lighthouse residence. He was planning to hide here as a joke and give Hatsue a scare when she came by. But as those sweet-sounding footsteps came closer and closer he became shy about frightening the girl. Instead, he deliberately let her know where he was by whistling a few lines from the Ise chorus she had been singing earlier:

*When the east is cloudy, they say the wind will blow;*
*When the west is cloudy, they say the rain will fall;*
*And even the largest ship . . .*

Hatsue rounded Woman's Slope, but her footsteps never paused. She walked right on past as though she had no idea Shinji was there.

"Hey! Hey!"

But still the girl did not look back. There was nothing to do but for him to walk silently along after her.

Entering the pine grove, the path became dark and steep. The girl was lighting her way with a small flashlight. Her steps became slower and, before she was aware of it, Shinji had taken the lead.

Suddenly the girl gave a little scream. The beam of the flashlight soared like a startled bird from the base of the pine trees up into the treetops.

The boy whirled around. Then he put his arms around

the girl, lying sprawled on the ground, and pulled her to her feet.

As he helped Hatsue up, the boy remembered with shame how he had lain in wait for her a while ago, had given that whistled signal, had followed after her: even though his actions had been prompted by the circumstances, to him they still seemed to smack of evil. Making no move to repeat yesterday's caress, he brushed the dirt off the girl's clothing as gently as though he were her big brother. The soil here was mostly dry sand and the dirt brushed off easily. Luckily there was no sign of any damage.

Hatsue stood motionless, like a child, resting her hand on Shinji's strong shoulder while he brushed her. Then she looked around for the flashlight, which she had dropped. It was lying on the ground behind them, still throwing its faint, fan-shaped beam, showing the ground covered with pine needles. The island's heavy twilight pressed in upon this single area of faint light.

"Look where it landed! I must have thrown it behind me when I fell." The girl spoke in a cheerful, laughing voice.

"What made you so mad?" Shinji asked, looking her full in the face.

"All that talk about you and Chiyoko-san."

"Stupid!"

"Then there's nothing to it?"

"There's nothing to it."

The two walked along side by side, Shinji holding the flashlight and guiding Hatsue along the difficult path as though he were a ship's pilot. There was nothing in particular to say, so the usually silent Shinji began to talk stumblingly to fill in the silence:

"As for me, some day I want to buy a coastal freighter with the money I've worked for and saved, and then go into the shipping business with my brother, carrying lumber from Kishu and coal from Kyushu. . . . Then I'll have my mother take it easy, and when I get old I'll come back to the island and take it easy too. . . . No matter where I sail, I'll never forget our island. . . . It has the most beautiful scenery in all Japan"—every person on Uta-jima was firmly convinced of this—"and in the same way I'll do my best to help make life on our island the most peaceful there is anywhere . . . the happiest there is anywhere. . . . Because if we don't do that, everybody will start forgetting the island and quit wanting to come back. No matter how much times change, very bad things —very bad ways—will all always disappear before they get to our island. . . . The sea—it only brings the good and right things that the island needs . . . and keeps the good and right things we already have here. . . . That's why there's not a thief on the whole island—nothing but brave, manly people—people who always have the will to work truly and well and put up with whatever comes— people whose love is never double-faced—people with nothing mean about them anywhere. . . ."

Of course the boy was not so articulate, and his way of speaking was confused and disconnected, but this is roughly what he told Hatsue in this moment of rare fluency.

She did not interrupt, but kept nodding her head in agreement with everything he said. Never once looking bored, her face overflowed with an expression of genuine sympathy and trust, all of which filled Shinji with joy.

Shinji did not want her to think he was being frivolous, and at the end of his serious speech he purposely omitted that last important hope that he had included in his prayer to the sea-god a few nights before.

There was nothing to hinder, and the path continued hiding them in the dense shadows of the trees, but this time Shinji did not even hold Hatsue's hand, much less dream of kissing her again. What had happened yesterday on the dark beach—to them that seemed not to have been an act of their own volition. It had been an undreamed-of event, brought about by some force outside themselves; it was a mystery how such a thing had come about. This time, they barely managed to make a date to meet again at the observation tower on the afternoon of the next time the fishing-boats could not go out.

When they emerged from the back of Yashiro Shrine, Hatsue gave a little gasp of admiration and stopped walking. Shinji stopped too.

The village was suddenly ablaze with brilliant lights. It was exactly like the opening of some spectacular, soundless festival: every window shone with a bright and indomitable light, a light without the slightest resemblance to the smoky light of oil lamps. It was as though the village had been restored to life and come floating up out of the black night. . . . The electric generator, so long out of order, had been repaired.

Outside the village they took different paths, and Hatsue went on alone down the stone steps and into the village, lit again, after such a long time, with street lamps.

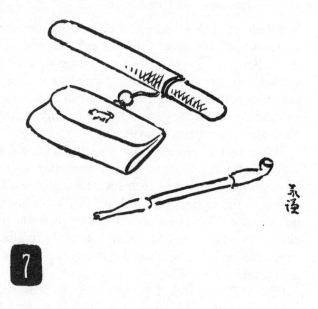

# 7

THE DAY CAME for Shinji's brother, Hiroshi, to go on the school excursion. They were to tour the Kyoto-Osaka area for six days, spending five nights away from home. This was the way the youths of Uta-jima, who had never before left the island, first saw the wide world outside with their own eyes, learning about it in a single gulp. In the same way, schoolboys of an earlier generation had crossed by boat to the mainland and stared with round eyes at the first horse-drawn omnibus they had ever seen, shouting: "Look! Look! A big dog pulling a privy!"

The children of the island got their first notions of the world outside from the pictures and words in their schoolbooks rather than from the real things. How difficult, then, for them to conceive, by sheer force of imagination, such things as streetcars, tall buildings, movies, subways,

But then, once they had seen reality, once the novelty of astonishment was gone, they perceived clearly how useless it had been for them to try to imagine such things, so much so that at the end of long lives spent on the island they would no longer even so much as remember the existence of such things as streetcars clanging back and forth along the streets of a city.

Before each school excursion Yashiro Shrine did a thriving business in talismans. In their everyday lives the island women committed their own bodies, as a matter of course, to the danger and the death that lurked in the sea, but when it came to excursions setting forth for gigantic cities they themselves had never seen, the mothers felt their children were embarking on great, death-defying adventures.

Hiroshi's mother had bought two precious eggs and made him a lunch of terribly salty fried eggs. And deep in his satchel, where he would not quickly find them, she had tucked away some caramels and fruit.

On that day alone the island's ferryboat, the *Kamikaze-maru*, left Uta-jima at the unusual hour of one in the afternoon. Formerly the stubborn old-timer who captained this putt-putt launch of something under twenty tons had refused as an abomination any departure from the established schedule. But then had come the year when his own son went on the excursion. Ever since then he had understood what they meant by saying the children would squander their money if the boat got to Toba too much ahead of time for their train to leave, and had grudgingly agreed to let the school authorities have their own way with the schedule.

The cabin and the deck of the *Kamikaze-maru* were

overflowing with schoolboys, satchels and canteens hanging across their breasts. The teachers in charge were terror-stricken by the swarm of mothers on the jetty. On Uta-jima a teacher's position depended upon the disposition of the mothers. One teacher had been branded a Communist by the mothers and driven off the island, while another, who was popular with the mothers, had even gotten one of the women teachers pregnant—and still been promoted to be acting assistant-principal.

It was the early afternoon of a truly springlike day, and as the boat set sail every mother was screaming the name of her own child. The boys, with the straps of their student-caps fixed under their chins, waited until they were sure their faces could no longer be distinguished from the shore and then began to yell back in high-spirited fun:

"Good-by, stupid! . . . Hooray! you old goose! . . . To hell with you! . . ."

The boat, jam-packed with black student-uniforms, kept throwing reflections of metal cap-badges and polished buttons back to shore until it was far out at sea. . . .

Once Hiroshi's mother was back, sitting on the straw mats of her own house, gloomy and deadly quiet even in the daytime, she began weeping, thinking of the day when both her sons would finally leave her for good and take to the sea.

The *Kamikaze-maru* had just discharged its load of students at the Toba pier opposite Mikimoto's "Pearl Island" and, regaining its usual happy-go-lucky, countrified air, was preparing for the return crossing to Uta-jima. There was a bucket atop the ancient smokestack, and water reflections were playing over the underside of the prow and over the great creels hanging from under the pier. A gray godown stood looking out across the sea, with the large white character for "Ice" painted on its side.

Chiyoko, the daughter of the lighthouse-keeper, was standing at the far end of the pier, holding a Boston bag. This unsociable girl, returning to the island after a long absence, disliked having the islanders greet and speak to her.

Chiyoko never wore a trace of make-up and her face was made all the more inconspicuous by the plain, dark-brown suit she was wearing. There was something about the cheerful, slapdash way her dingy features were thrown together that might have appealed to some. But she always wore a gloomy expression and, in her constantly perverse way, insisted upon thinking of herself as unattractive. Until now this was the most noticeable result of the "refinements" she was learning at the university in Tokyo. But probably the way she brooded over her commonplace face as being so unlovely was just as presumptuous as if she had been convinced she was an utter beauty.

Chiyoko's good-natured father had also contributed, unwittingly, to this gloomy conviction of hers. She was always complaining so openly that she had inherited her ugliness from him that, even when she was in the next room, the outspoken lighthouse-keeper would grumble to his guests:

"Well, there's no doubt about this grown-up daughter of mine being homely. It really makes me sad. I'm so ugly myself that I guess I have to take the blame for it. But then, I suppose that's fate."

.   .   .

Someone clapped Chiyoko on the shoulder and she turned around. It was Yasuo Kawamoto, the president of the Young Men's Association. He stood there laughing, his leather jacket glistening in the sun.

"Ho! Welcome home. Spring vacation, isn't it?"

"Yes. Exams were over yesterday."

"So now we've come back to have another drink of mother's milk?"

The day before, Yasuo's father had sent him to attend to some business for the Co-operative with the prefectural authorities at Tsu. He had spent the night at an inn in Toba run by relatives and now was taking the boat back to Uta-jima. He took great pride in showing this girl from a Tokyo university how well he could speak, without any trace of island dialect.

Chiyoko was conscious of the masculine joviality of this young man her own age; his worldly manner seemed to be saying: "There's no doubt but what this girl has a fancy for me." This feeling made her even more bad-tempered.

"Here it is again!" she told herself. Influenced both by her natural disposition and by the movies seen and novels read in Tokyo, she was always wishing that she could have a man look at her at least once with eyes saying "I love you" instead of "You love me." But she had decided she would never have such an experience in all her life.

A loud, rough voice shouted from the *Kamikaze-maru*:

"Hey! Where the blazes is that load of quilts? Somebody find them!"

Soon a man came carrying a great bale of arabesque-patterned quilts on his shoulders. They had been lying on the quay, half hidden in the shadows of the godown.

"The boat's about ready to leave," Yasuo said.

As they jumped from the pier to the deck, Yasuo took Chiyoko's hand and helped her across. Chiyoko thought how different his iron-like hand felt from the hands of men in Tokyo. But in her imagination it was Shinji's hand she was feeling—a hand she had never even so much as shaken.

Peering down through the small hatchway into the murky passenger cabin, all the more darkly stagnant to their daylight-accustomed eyes, they could barely make out, from the white towels tied around their necks or the occasional flickering reflection from a pair of spectacles, the forms of people lolling on the straw matting.

"It's better on deck. Even if it's a bit cold, it's still better."

Yasuo and Chiyoko took shelter from the wind behind the wheelhouse and sat down, leaning against a coil of rope.

The captain's snappish young helper came up and said: "Hey! How's about lifting your asses a minute?"

With that, he pulled a plank out from under them. They had sat down on the hatch used for closing the passenger cabin.

Up in the wheelhouse, where scruffy, peeling paint half revealed the grain of the wood underneath, the captain rang the ship's bell. . . . The *Kamikaze-maru* was under way.

Surrendering their bodies to the shuddering of the ancient engine, Yasuo and Chiyoko gazed back at Toba's receding harbor. Yasuo very much wanted to drop a hint about how he had slipped off and bought himself a piece last night, but decided he had better not. If he had been a boy from an ordinary farming or fishing village, his experience with women would have been cause for boasting, but on strait-laced Uta-jima he had to keep his mouth tightly shut. Young as he was, he had already learned to play the hypocrite.

Chiyoko was betting with herself as to the instant when a sea gull would fly even higher than the steel tower of the cableway that ascended the mountain behind Toba station. This girl who, out of shyness, had never had any sort of adventures in Tokyo, had been hoping that when she returned to the island something wonderful would happen to her, something that would completely change her world.

Once the boat was well away from Toba harbor, it would be an easy matter for even the lowest-flying gulls to seem to rise higher than the receding steel tower. But right now the tower was still soaring high in the air. Chiyoko looked closely at the second-hand of her wrist watch, fastened with its red-leather strap.

"If a sea gull flies higher than that within the next thirty seconds, that'll mean something wonderful really is waiting for me."

Five seconds passed. . . . A sea gull that had come following alongside the boat suddenly flew high into the air, flapping its wings—and rose higher than the tower!

Afraid that the boy at her side might remark on her smile, Chiyoko broke her long silence:

"Is there any news on the island?"

The boat was passing Sakate Island to port. Yasuo's cigarette had become so short it was burning his lips. He crushed the butt out on the deck and answered:

"Nothing in particular. . . . Oh, yes, the generator was broken down until ten days ago and the whole village was using lamps. But it's fixed now."

"Yes, my mother wrote me about that."

"Oh, she did? Well, as for any more news . . ."

Yasuo narrowed his eyes against the glare of the sea, which was overflowing with the light of spring. The Coast Guard cutter *Hiyodori-maru* was passing them at a distance of about ten yards, sailing in the direction of Toba.

". . . Oh, I forgot. Uncle Teru Miyata has brought his daughter back home. Her name's Hatsue, and she's a real beauty."

"So?"

Chiyoko's face had clouded at the word "beauty." Just the word alone seemed an implied criticism of her own looks.

"I'm a great favorite of Uncle Teru's, all right. And there's my older brother to carry on our own family. So everybody in the village is saying I'm sure to be chosen for Hatsue's husband and adopted into her family."

Soon the *Kamikaze-maru* had brought Suga Island into view to starboard, and Toshi Island to port. No matter how calm the weather, once a boat passed beyond the protection of these two islands, high-running waves would always set the boat's timbers to creaking. From this point on they saw numerous cormorants floating in the wave-troughs and, farther out to sea, the many rocks of Oki Shallows projecting up above the water.

Yasuo knitted his brows and averted his eyes from the sight of Oki Shallows, the reminder of Uta-jima's one and only humiliation. Fishing rights in these shallows, where the blood of Uta-jima's youth had been shed in ancient rivalries, had now been restored to Toshi Island.

Chiyoko and Yasuo got to their feet and, looking across the low wheelhouse, waited for the shape of an island that would soon appear in the ocean before them. . . .

As always, Uta-jima rose from the level of the sea shaped like some amorphous, mysterious helmet.

The boat tilted—and the helmet seemed to tilt with it.

## 8

A DAY OF REST from fishing seemed never to come. Finally, two days after Hiroshi left on the school excursion, the island was struck by such a storm that no boats could put out. It seemed that not one of the island's meager cherry blossoms, just then beginning to open, could escape destruction.

On the previous day an unseasonably damp wind had enveloped and clung to the sails, and at sunset a strange light had spread over the sky. A ground swell set in; the beach was aroar with incoming waves; the sea-lice and dango bugs scurried for high ground. During the night a high wind came blowing, mixed with rain, and the heavens and the sea were filled with sounds like human shrieks and shrilling fifes. . . .

· · ·

Shinji listened to the voice of the storm from his pallet. It was enough to tell him the boats would not put out today. This would be too much even for braiding rope or repairing fishing tackle, perhaps too much even for the Young Men's Association's rat-catching project.

Not wanting to waken his mother, whose breathing from the next pallet told him she was still asleep, Shinji thoughtfully kept still, waiting eagerly for the first grayness at the window. The house was shaking violently and the windows were rattling. Somewhere a sheet of tin fell with a great clatter. The houses on Uta-jima, the big rich houses as well as the tiny one-story houses such as Shinji's, were all built alike, with the entrance into a dirt-floored work-room, flanked by the toilet-room on the left and the kitchen on the right; and amid the wind's fury, in the pre-dawn blackness, there was a single odor that dominated the entire house, hanging quietly on the air inside —that darkish, cold, meditative odor of the toilet-room.

The window, which faced the wall of the next-door neighbor's storehouse, slowly turned gray. Shinji looked up at the pouring rain, beating upon the eaves and spreading wetly across the windowpanes. Before, he had hated days when there was no fishing, days that robbed him both of the pleasure of working and of income, but now the prospect of such a day seemed the most wonderful of festival days to him. It was a festival made glorious, not with blue skies and flags waving from poles topped with golden balls, but with a storm, raging seas, and a wind that shrieked as it came tearing through the prostrate treetops.

Finding it unbearable to wait, the boy leaped from bed and jerked on a pair of trousers and a black, crew-neck sweater full of holes.

A moment later his mother awakened to see the dark shadow of a man against the window, faintly lit with dawn.

"Hey! Who's there?" she shouted.

"Me."

"Oh . . . don't scare me so! Today, in weather like this, you're going fishing?"

"The boats won't be going out, but . . ."

"Well, then, why not sleep a little longer? Why, I thought it was some stranger at the window!"

The mother was not far wrong in the first thought she had had upon opening her eyes: her son did indeed seem a stranger this morning. Here he was, this Shinji who almost never opened his mouth, singing at the top of his voice and making a show of gymnastics by swinging from the door-lintel.

Not knowing the reason for her son's strange behavior and fearing he would pull the house down, his mother grumbled:

"If it's a storm outside, what else is it we've got right here inside the house?"

Countless times Shinji went to peer up at the sooty clock on the wall. With a heart unaccustomed to doubting, he never wondered for an instant whether the girl would brave such a storm to keep their rendezvous. He knew nothing of that melancholy and all-too-effective way of passing time by magnifying and complicating his feelings, whether of happiness or uneasiness, through the exercise of the imagination.

When he could no longer bear the thought of waiting, Shinji flung on a rubber raincoat and went down to meet the sea. It seemed to him that only the sea would be kind enough to answer his wordless conversation.

Raging waves rose high above the breakwater, set up a tremendous roar, and then rushed on down. Because of the previous evening's storm-warning, every last boat had been pulled up much higher on the beach than usual. When the giant waves receded, the surface of the water tilted steeply; it almost seemed as if the bottom of the sea inside the harbor-works would be exposed to view.

Spray from the waves, mixed with the driving rain, struck Shinji full in the face. The sharp, fresh saltiness ran down his flushed cheeks, down the lines of his nose, and Shinji recalled the taste of Hatsue's lips.

The clouds were moving at a gallop, and even in the dark sky there was a restless fluctuation between light and dark. Once in a while, still deeper in the sky, Shinji caught glimpses of clouds charged with an opaque light, like promises of clear skies to come. But these would be effaced almost instantly.

Shinji was so intent upon the sky that a wave came right up to where he stood and wet the toe-thongs of his wooden clogs. At his feet there lay a beautiful small pink shell, apparently just washed up by the same wave.

He picked the shell up and examined it. It was perfectly formed, without even the slightest chip on its paper-thin edge. Deciding it would make a good present, he put it in his pocket.

Immediately after lunch Shinji began getting ready to go out again. Seeing him going out into the storm for a second time, the mother paused in her dishwashing to stare fixedly after him. But she did not venture to ask where he was going: there was something about her son's back that warned her to keep silent. How she regretted she had not had at least one daughter, who would always have been at home to help with the housework. . . .

Men go out fishing. They board their coasting ships and carry cargo to all sorts of ports. Women, not destined for that wide world, cook rice, draw water, gather seaweed, and when summer comes dive into the water, down to the sea's deep bottom. Even for a mother who was a veteran among diving women this twilight world of the sea's bottom was the world of women. . . .

All this she knew. The interior of a house dark even at noon, the somber pangs of childbirth, the gloom at the bottom of the sea—these were the series of interrelated worlds in which she lived her life.

The mother remembered one of the women of the summer before last, a widow like herself, a frail woman still carrying a nursing child. The woman had come up from diving for abalone, and had suddenly fallen unconscious as she stood before the drying-fire. She had turned up the whites of her eyes, bitten her blue lips, and dropped to the ground. When her remains were cremated at twilight in the pine grove, the other diving women had been filled with such grief that they could not stand, but squatted on the ground, weeping.

A strange story had been told about that incident, and some of the women had become afraid to dive any more. It was said that the dead woman had been punished for having seen a fearful something at the bottom of the sea, a something that humans are not meant to see.

Shinji's mother had scoffed at the story and had dived to greater and greater depths to bring up the biggest catches of the season. She had never been one to worry about unknown things. . . .

Even such recollections as these could not dent her natural cheerfulness: she felt boastful about her own good health, and the storm outside quickened her feeling of well-being, just as it had her son's.

Finishing the dishwashing, she opened wide the skirts of her kimono and sat down with her bare legs stretched out in front of her, gazing at them earnestly in the dim light from the creaking windows. There was not a single wrinkle on the sunburnt, well-ripened thighs, their wonderfully rounded flesh all but gleaming with the color of amber.

"Like this, I could still have four or five children more." But at the thought her virtuous heart became filled with contrition.

Quickly tidying her clothing, she bowed before her husband's memorial tablet.

The path the boy followed up to the lighthouse had been turned into a mountain torrent by the rain, washing away his footprints. The tops of the pine trees howled. His rubber boots made walking difficult and, as he carried no umbrella, he could feel the rain running down his close-cropped hair and into his collar. But he kept on climbing, his face to the storm. He was not defying the storm; instead, in exactly the same way that he felt a quiet happiness when surrounded by the quietness of nature, his feelings now were in complete concord with nature's present fury.

He looked down through the pine thicket at the sea, where countless whitecaps were tearing in. From time to time even the high rocks at the tip of the promontory were covered by the waves.

Passing Woman's Slope, Shinji could see the one-storied

lighthouse residence kneeling in the storm, all its windows closed, its curtains drawn fast. He climbed on up the stone steps toward the lighthouse.

There was no sign of a watchman within the fast-shut watchhouse. Inside the glass doors, which streamed with driven rain and rattled ceaselessly, there stood the telescope, turned blankly toward the closed windows. There were papers scattered from the desk by the drafts, a pipe, a regulation Coast Guard cap, the calendar of a steamship company showing a gaudy painting of a new ship, and on the same wall with the calendar a pair of drafting triangles hanging nonchalantly from a nail.

Shinji arrived at the observation tower drenched to the skin. The storm was all the more fearful at such a deserted place. Here, almost at the summit of the island, with nothing to intervene between naked sky and earth, the storm could be seen reigning in supreme dominion.

The ruined building, its windows gaping wide in three directions, gave not the slightest protection against the wind. Rather, it seemed as though the tower were inviting the tempest into its rooms, and there abandoning it to the revel. The immense view of the Pacific from the second-floor windows was reduced in sweep by the rain clouds, but the way the waves, raging and ripping out their white linings on every hand, faded off into the encircling black clouds made the turbulent expanse seem instead to be boundless.

The boy went back down the outside staircase and peered into the room on the ground floor where he had come before to get his mother's firewood. It had apparently been used originally as a storehouse, and its windows were so tiny that only one of them had been broken.

He saw that it offered ideal shelter. The mountain of pine needles that had been there before had apparently been carried away bale by bale until now only four or five bales remained in a far corner.

"It's like a jail," Shinji thought, noticing the moldy odor.

No sooner had he taken shelter from the storm than he was suddenly conscious of a wet-cold feeling. He sneezed hugely. Taking off his raincoat, he felt in the pockets of his trousers for the matches that life at sea had taught him always to carry with him.

Before he found the matches his fingers touched the shell he had picked up on the beach that morning. He took it out now and held it up toward the light of a window. The pink shell was gleaming lustrously, as though it might have been still wet with sea water. Satisfied, the boy returned the shell to his pocket.

He gathered dried pine needles and brushwood from a broken bale, heaped them on the cement floor, and with much difficulty succeeded in lighting one of the damp matches. Then for a time the room was completely filled with smoke, until at last the dismal smoldering broke into a tiny flame and began to flicker.

The boy took off his sodden trousers and hung them near the fire to dry. Then he sat down before the fire and clasped his knees. Now there was nothing to do but wait. . . .

Shinji waited. Without the slightest uneasiness he whiled away the time by poking his fingers into the holes in his black sweater, making them still larger.

He became lost in the sensations of his body as it gradually became warm, and in the voice of the storm outside; he surrendered himself to the euphoria created by his trusting devotion itself. The fact that he was lacking in the ability to imagine all sorts of things that might keep the girl from coming did not trouble him in the least.

And thus it was that he laid his head on his knees and fell asleep.

When Shinji opened his eyes, the blazing fire was there before him, burning as brightly as ever, as though he had only closed his eyes the moment before. But a strange, indistinct shadow was standing across the fire from him. He wondered if he were dreaming.

It was a naked girl who stood there, her head bent low, holding a white chemise to dry at the fire. Standing as she was, the chemise held down toward the fire with both hands, she was revealing the whole upper half of her body.

When he realized that this was certainly no dream, the idea occurred to Shinji that, by using just a little cunning and pretending to be still asleep, he could watch her through half-closed eyes. And yet, her body was almost too beautiful to be watched without moving at all.

Diving women are accustomed to drying their entire bodies at a fire upon coming out of the water. Hence Hatsue had apparently not given the matter a second thought upon doing so now. When she arrived at the meeting place, there the fire was, and there the boy was— fast asleep. So, making up her mind as quickly as a child, she evidently had decided to waste no time in drying her wet clothes and her wet body while the boy slept. In short, the idea that she was undressing in front of a man

72

had never crossed her mind. She was simply undressing before a fire—because this happened to be the only fire there was, because she was wet.

If Shinji had had more experience with women, as he looked at the naked Hatsue standing there across the fire, in the storm-encircled ruins, he would have seen unmistakably that hers was the body of a virgin. Her skin, far from fair-complexioned, had been constantly bathed in sea-water and stretched smooth; and there, upon the wide expanse of a chest that had served for many long dives, two small, firm breasts turned their faces slightly away from each other, as though abashed, and lifted up two rose-colored buds. Since Shinji, fearful of being discovered, had barely opened his eyes, the girl's form remained a vague outline and, peered at through a fire that reached as high as the concrete ceiling, became almost indistinguishable from the wavering flames themselves.

But then the boy happened to blink his eyes, and for an instant the shadow of his lashes, magnified by the firelight, moved across his cheeks.

Quick as thought, the girl hid her breasts with the white chemise, not yet completely dry, and cried out:

"Keep your eyes shut!"

The honest boy immediately clamped his eyes tightly shut. Now that he thought about it, it had certainly been wrong of him to pretend to be still sleeping. . . . But then, was it his fault that he had waked up when he did? Taking courage from this just and fair reasoning, for a second time he opened wide his black, beautiful eyes.

Completely at a loss as to what to do, the girl still had not even so much as started putting on her chemise.

73

Again she cried out in a sharp, childlike voice:

"Keep your eyes shut!"

But the boy no longer made the slightest pretense at closing his eyes. Ever since he could remember, he had been used to seeing the women of this fishing village naked, but this was the first time he had ever seen the girl he loved naked. And yet he could not understand why, just because she was naked, a barrier should have risen between them, making difficult the everyday civilities, the matter-of-course familiarities. With the straightforwardness of youth, he rose to his feet.

The boy and girl faced each other then, separated by the flames.

The boy moved slightly to the right. The girl retreated a little to the right also. And there the fire was, between them, forever.

"What are you running away for?"

"Why, because I'm ashamed."

The boy did not say: "Then why don't you put your clothes on?" If only for a little longer, he wanted to look at her. Then, feeling he must say something, he burst out with a childish question:

"What would make you quit being ashamed?"

To this the girl gave a truly naïve answer, though a startling one:

"If you took your clothes off too, then I wouldn't be ashamed."

Now Shinji was at a complete loss. But after an instant's hesitation he began taking off his crew-neck sweater, saying not a word. Struck by the thought that Hatsue might run away while he was undressing, he kept a lookout that was scarcely broken even during the instant when the sweater passed over his face. Then his nimble hands had the sweater off and thrown aside, and there stood the naked figure of a young man—far handsomer than when dressed—wearing only a narrow loincloth, his thoughts turned so ardently upon the girl opposite him that for the moment his body had completely lost its sense of shame.

"Now you're not ashamed any more, are you?" He flung the question at her as though cross-examining a witness.

Without realizing the enormity of what she was saying, the girl gave an amazing explanation:

"Yes . . ."

"Why?"

"You—you still haven't taken everything off."

Now the sense of shame returned, and in the firelight the boy's body flushed crimson. He started to speak—and choked on the words. Then, drawing so near the fire that his fingertips were all but burned, and staring at the girl's chemise, which the flames set swaying with shadows, Shinji finally managed to speak:

"If—if you'll take that away—I will too."

Hatsue broke into a spontaneous smile. But neither she nor Shinji had the slightest idea what the meaning of her smile might be.

The white chemise in the girl's hands had been half covering her body, from breast to thigh. Now she flung it away behind her.

The boy saw her, and then, standing just as he was, like some piece of heroic sculpture, never taking his eyes from the girl's, he untied his loincloth.

At this moment the storm suddenly planted its feet wide and firmly outside the windows. All along, the wind and rain had been raging madly around the ruins with the same force as now, but in this instant the boy and girl realized the certainty of the storm's existence, realized that directly beneath the high windows the wide Pacific was shaking with everlasting frenzy.

The girl took a few steps backward. . . . There was no way out. The sooty concrete wall touched her back.

"Hatsue!" the boy cried.

"Jump across the fire to me. Come on! If you'll jump across the fire to me . . ." The girl was breathing hard, but her voice came clearly, firmly.

The naked boy did not hesitate an instant. He sprang from tiptoe and his body, shining in the flames, came flying at full speed into the fire. In the next instant he was directly in front of the girl. His chest lightly touched her breasts.

"Firm softness—this is the firm softness that I imagined the other day under that red sweater," he thought in a turmoil.

They were in each other's arms. The girl was the first to sink limply to the floor, pulling the boy after her.

"Pine needles—they hurt," the girl said.

The boy reached out for the white chemise and tried to pull it under the girl's body.

She stopped him. Her arms were no longer embracing him. She drew her knees up, crushed the chemise into a ball in her hands, thrust it down below her waist, and exactly like a child who has just thrown cupped hands over an insect in the bushes, doggedly protected her body with it.

The words which Hatsue spoke next were weighted with virtue:

"It's bad. It's bad! . . . It's bad for a girl to do that before she's married."

"You really think it's so bad?" the crestfallen boy asked, without any conviction.

"It's bad." As the girl's eyes were closed, she could speak without hesitation, in a tone of voice that seemed to be both reproving and placating. "It's bad for *now*. Because I've decided it's you I'm going to marry, and until I do, it's really bad."

Shinji had a sort of haphazard respect for moral things. And even more because he had never yet known a woman, he believed he had now penetrated to the moralistic core of woman's being. He insisted no further.

The boy's arms were still embracing the girl. They could hear each other's naked throbbing. A long kiss tortured the unsatisfied boy, but then at a certain instant this pain was transformed into a strange elation.

From time to time the dying fire crackled a little. They heard this sound and the whistling of the storm as it swept past the high windows, all mixed with the beating of their hearts. To Shinji it seemed as though this unceasing feeling of intoxication, and the confused booming of the sea outside, and the noise of the storm among the treetops were all beating with nature's violent rhythm. And as part of his emotion there was the feeling, forever and ever, of pure and holy happiness.

He moved his body away from hers. Then he spoke in a manly, composed tone of voice:

"Today on the beach I found a pretty shell and brought it for you."

"Oh, thanks—let me see it."

Getting up, Shinji went to where his clothes had fallen

and began putting them on. At the same time Hatsue softly pulled on her chemise and then put on the rest of her clothes.

After they were both fully dressed, the boy brought the shell to where the girl was sitting.

"My, it *is* pretty." Delighted, the girl mirrored the flames in the smooth face of the shell. Then she held it up against her hair and said:

"It looks like coral, doesn't it? Wonder if it wouldn't even make a pretty hair ornament?"

Shinji sat down on the floor close beside the girl.

Now that they were dressed, they could kiss in comfort. . . .

When they started back, the storm still had not abated, so this time Shinji did not part from her above the lighthouse, did not take a different path out of deference to what the people in the lighthouse might think. Instead, together they followed the slightly easier path that led down past the rear of the lighthouse. Then, arm in arm, they descended the stone stairs leading from the lighthouse past the residence.

Chiyoko had come home, and by the next day was overcome with boredom. Not even Shinji came to see her. Finally a regular meeting of the etiquette class brought the village girls to the house.

There was an unfamiliar face among them. Chiyoko realized this must be the Hatsue of whom Yasuo had spoken, and she found Hatsue's rustic features even more beautiful than the islanders said they were. This was an odd virtue of Chiyoko's: although a woman with the slightest degree of self-confidence will never cease pointing out another woman's defects, Chiyoko was even more honest than a man in always recognizing anything beautiful about any woman except herself.

With nothing better to do, Chiyoko had begun studying her history of English literature. Knowing not a single one of their works, she memorized the names of a group of Victorian lady poets—Christina Georgina Rossetti, Adelaide Anne Procter, Jean Ingelow, Augusta Webster—exactly as though she were memorizing Buddhist scriptures. Rote memorization was Chiyoko's forte; even the professor's sneezes were recorded in her notes.

Her mother was constantly at her side, eager to gain new knowledge from her daughter. Going to the university had been Chiyoko's idea in the first place, but it had been her mother's enthusiastic support that had overcome her father's reluctance.

Her thirst for knowledge whetted by a life of moving from lighthouse to lighthouse, from remote island to remote island, the mother always pictured her daughter's life as an ideal dream. Never once did her eyes perceive her daughter's little inner unhappinesses.

On the morning of the storm both mother and daughter slept late. The storm had been building up since the evening before, and they had kept vigil most of the night with the lighthouse-keeper, who took his responsibilities most seriously. Very much contrary to their usual ways, their midday meal was also their breakfast. And after the table had been cleared, the three of them passed the time quietly indoors, shut in by the storm.

Chiyoko began to long for Tokyo. She longed for the Tokyo where, even on such a stormy day, the automobiles went back and forth as usual, the elevators went up and down, and the streetcars bustled along. There in the city almost all nature had been put into uniform, and the little power of nature that remained was an enemy. Here on the island, however, the islanders enthusiastically entered into an alliance with nature and gave it their full support.

Bored with studying, Chiyoko pressed her face against a windowpane and gazed out at the storm that kept her shut up in the house. The storm was a monotone of dullness. The roar of the waves came as persistently as the garrulity of a drunk man.

For some reason Chiyoko recalled the gossip about a classmate who had been seduced by the man she was in love with. The girl had loved the man for his gentleness and refinement, and had even said so openly. After that night, so the story went, she loved him for his violence and willfulness—but this she never breathed to anyone. . . .

At this moment Chiyoko caught sight of Shinji descending the storm-swept stairs—with Hatsue snuggled against him.

Chiyoko was convinced of the advantages of a face as ugly as she believed her own to be: once such a face hardened in its mold, it could hide emotions far more cleverly than could a beautiful one. What she regarded as ugly, however, was actually only the plaster-of-Paris mask of self-preoccupied virginity.

She turned away from the window. Beside the sunken hearth her mother was sewing and her father was silently smoking his New Life. Outdoors was the storm; indoors, domesticity. Nowhere was there anyone to heed Chiyoko's unhappiness.

Chiyoko returned to her desk and opened the English book. The words had no meaning; there was nothing but the lines of type running down the page. Between the lines the vision of birds wheeling high and low flickered in her eyes. They were sea gulls.

"When I returned to the island," Chiyoko told herself, "and made that bet about a sea gull flying over Toba's tower—*this* is what the sign meant. . . ."

# 9

A MESSAGE CAME by express delivery from Hiroshi on his trip. It was written on a picture postcard showing Kyoto's famous Kiyomizu Temple and was impressed with a large, purple souvenir seal. If he had sent it by ordinary mail, he himself would probably have been back on the island before it arrived. Even before reading it, his mother became angry, saying that Hiroshi had been extravagant to pay all that extra postage, that children nowadays didn't know the value of money.

Hiroshi's closely written card was all about seeing his first motion picture, with not so much as a word about the famous scenic spots and historic places he was seeing:

*"The first night in Kyoto they let us do as we pleased, so Sochan, Katchan, and I went straight to a big movie-*

*house in the neighborhood. It was really swell—just like a palace. But the seats seemed awful narrow and hard, and when we tried to sit on them it was just like perching on a chicken roost. Our bottoms hurt so that we couldn't get comfortable at all.*

*"After a few minutes the man behind us yelled: 'Down in front! Down in front!' We were already sitting down, so we thought this was funny. But then the man very kindly showed us what to do. He said they were folding seats, and that if we'd turn them down, they'd become chairs. We all scratched our heads, knowing we'd made a foolish mistake. And when we put them down, sure enough they were seats soft enough for the Emperor himself to sit on. I told myself that some day I'd like to have Mother sit on these seats too."*

As Shinji read the card aloud for his mother, that last sentence brought tears to her eyes. She put the card up on the god-shelf and made Shinji kneel down with her to pray that the storm two days before had not interfered with Hiroshi's excursion and that nothing would happen to him before he came home the day after tomorrow.

After a minute, as though the thought had just occurred to her, she started heaping Shinji with abuse, going on about how terrible his reading and writing were and how much smarter Hiroshi was than he. What she called Hiroshi's smartness was nothing more or less than his ability to make her shed happy tears.

She wasted no time in hurrying off to show the post-card at the homes of Hiroshi's friends Sochan and Katchan. Later that evening, when she and Shinji went to the public bath, she met the postmaster's wife, and she got down on her bare knees in the midst of the steam to

bow and thank her because the express delivery had been
made in such good order.

Shinji soon finished his bathing and waited before the
bathhouse entrance for his mother to come out of the
women's side. The carved and painted wood under the
eaves of the bathhouse was faded and peeling where the
steam came curling out. The night was warm, the sea
calm.

Shinji noticed someone standing a few yards farther
along the street, his back turned in Shinji's direction, apparently looking up toward the eaves of one of the houses.
The man stood with both hands in his pockets and was
beating time on the flagstones with his wooden clogs. In
the twilight Shinji could see that he was wearing a brown
leather jacket. On Uta-jima it was not everyone who
could afford a leather jacket, and Shinji was sure this was
Yasuo.

Just as Shinji was about to call out to him, Yasuo happened to turn around. Shinji smiled. But Yasuo only
stared back at him, the blank expression on his face never
changing, and then turned away again.

Shinji did not particularly take this as a slight, but it did
seem a bit odd. Just then his mother came out of the bathhouse, and the boy walked along home with her, silent
as usual.

The day before, after the boats had returned from a day
of fishing in the fine weather that followed the storm,
Chiyoko had gone to see Yasuo. She said she had come to
the village shopping with her mother and had decided to
drop by, and explained her coming to Yasuo's place alone

by saying her mother was visiting the home of the head of the Co-operative, which was near by.

Chiyoko's version of how she had seen Shinji and Hatsue coming down together from the deserted mountain, clinging to each other, certainly did nothing to make the event less compromising; and her story was a staggering blow to Yasuo's pride. He brooded about it all night. And the next night, when Shinji happened to see him, what he was actually doing was reading the roster displayed under the eaves of a house beside the steep street that ran through the center of the village.

Uta-jima had a meager water supply, which reached its lowest point about the time of the old-calendar New Year, leading to endless quarrels over water rights. The village's sole source of water was a narrow stream beside the cobbled street that tumbled in flights of steps down through the center of the village. During the wet season or after a heavy rain the stream would become a muddy torrent, on whose banks the village women would do their laundry, chattering together noisily. Here too the children would hold the launching ceremonies for their hand-carved warships. But during the dry season the stream would all but become a dried-up marsh, without strength enough to wash away even the slightest bit of rubbish.

The stream was fed by a spring. Perhaps it was because the rains that fell on the peaks of the island all filtered down to this spring, but whatever the cause, this was the only such spring on the island. Hence the village government had long since been given the power of determining the order in which the villagers should draw their water, the order being rotated each week.

Only the lighthouse filtered rain water and stored it in

a tank; all the other houses on the island depended solely upon this spring, and each family in its turn had to put up with the inconvenience of being assigned the midnight hours for water drawing. But after a few weeks even a midnight turn would gradually move up the roster to the convenient hours of early morning. Drawing water was women's work.

So Yasuo was looking up at the water-drawing roster, posted where the most people passed. He found the name Miyata written precisely under the 2 A.M. column. This was Hatsue's turn.

Yasuo clicked his tongue. He wished it were still octopus season, as the boats did not put out quite so early in the morning then. During the squid season, which had now arrived, the boats had to reach the fishing grounds in the Irako Channel by the crack of dawn. So every household was up preparing breakfast by three o'clock at the latest, and impatient houses were sending up smoke from their cooking fires even earlier.

Even so, this was preferable to next week, when Hatsue's turn would come at three o'clock. . . . Yasuo swore to himself that he would have Hatsue before the fishing-boats put out the next morning.

Standing looking at the roster, he had just made this firm resolve when he saw Shinji standing before the men's entrance to the bathhouse. The sight of Shinji annoyed him so that he completely forgot his usual punctilious ways and turned his back to hurry home.

Reaching home, Yasuo glanced out of the corner of his eye into the sitting-room, where his father and elder brother were still serving each other their evening saké and listening to a ballad singer on the radio, which was resounding throughout the house. Yasuo went straight on to his own room on the second floor, where he angrily puffed on a cigarette.

Because of his experience and way of thinking, Yasuo saw the matter thus: As Shinji had seduced Hatsue, he had certainly been no virgin. All the time he had been coming to the meetings of the Young Men's Association, sitting there innocently clasping his knees, smiling and listening attentively to the others' talk, putting on his childish airs—all that time he'd been having women on the sly. The damn little fox!

And yet, given the honesty of Shinji's face, even Yasuo simply could not believe him capable of having won the girl by deceit. The inevitable conclusion then—and this was the most unbearable thought of all—was that Shinji had had his way with the girl fairly and squarely, with complete honesty.

In bed that night Yasuo kept pinching his thighs to keep from going to sleep. But this was not really necessary: the animosity he felt toward Shinji and the jealousy he felt at Shinji's having stolen a march on him were enough to keep him awake of themselves.

Yasuo was the proud and always bragging owner of a watch with a luminous dial. Tonight he had left this on his wrist and had slipped into bed still wearing his jacket and trousers. From time to time he put the watch to his ear, looking often at its luminously glowing face. In Yasuo's opinion the mere ownership of such a wonderful watch made him by rights a favorite with the women.

At twenty minutes past one Yasuo stole out of the

house. In the dead of night the sound of the waves could be plainly heard, and the moon was shining brightly. The village was silent.

There were only four street lamps on the island—one at the jetty, two along the steep street through the center of the village, and one on the mountain beside the spring. Except for the ferryboat there were nothing but fishing-boats in the harbor, so there were no masthead lights to enliven the night there, and every last light in the houses had been turned off. Moreover, here in a fishing village where the roofs were made of tile or galvanized iron, there were none of those rows of thick, black roofs that seem so imposing at night in a farm village; there was none of the solemn weightiness of thatch to intimidate and hold back the night.

Yasuo quickly mounted the sloping street to the right, his sneakers making not so much as a footfall. He passed through the playground of the elementary school, enclosed in rows of cherry trees, their blossoms half-open. This playground was a recent addition to the school, and the cherry trees had been transplanted from the mountains. One of the young trees had been blown over by the storm; its trunk showed dead-black against a moonlit sand pile.

Yasuo climbed the stone steps beside the stream until he reached a spot where he could hear the sound of the spring. In the light of the solitary street lamp he could see the outlines of the spring.

Clear water flowed out from between moss-covered rocks, into a stone cistern, and then brimmed over one edge of the stone. The stone there was covered with glossy moss, and it seemed, not that water was flowing down over the moss, but that the moss had been thickly coated with some beautiful transparent enamel. From some-

88

where in the thicket around the spring an owl was hoot-
ing.

Yasuo hid himself behind the lamp-post. There was a
tiny flutter of wings taking flight. Yasuo leaned against a
huge beech tree and waited, trying to outstare the luminous eyes of his watch.

Soon it was two o'clock and Yasuo caught sight of Hatsue coming across the schoolyard, carrying a water bucket
on either end of a wooden pole across her shoulders. Her
outline was sharply etched in the moonlight.

Although a woman's body is ill-suited for midnight
labor, on Uta-jima men and women alike, rich and poor,
had to perform their own tasks. Robust Hatsue, hardened
by the life of a diving woman, came up the stone steps
without the slightest difficulty, swinging the empty pails
to and fro and giving rather the merry appearance of actually enjoying her untimely work.

At long last Hatsue had put her buckets down beside the
spring. This was the moment when Yasuo had intended
to jump out at her, but now he hesitated and decided to
hold back until she had finished drawing her water. Preparing to leap out when the moment came, he reached
up and caught hold of a high branch with his left hand.
Then he stood perfectly still, imagining himself to be a
stone statue. He watched the girl's strong hands, red and
slightly frostbitten, as she filled the buckets, splashing the
water about with lush sounds, and the sight quickened
his imagination with delightfully carnal pictures of her
healthy young body.

All the time the luminous watch of which Yasuo was
so proud, strapped above the hand with which he was
holding onto the branch of the beech tree, was giving off

its phosphorescent glow, faintly but distinctly ticking away the seconds. This aroused a swarm of hornets in the nest fastened to this same branch and greatly excited their curiosity.

One of the hornets came flying timidly toward the wrist watch, only to find that this strange beetle that emitted a shimmering light and chirruped methodically was protected within slippery, cold armour of glass. Perhaps out of disappointment, the hornet turned its stinger toward the skin at Yasuo's wrist—and drove it in with all its might.

Yasuo gave a shout.

Hatsue straightened up and turned in his direction, but she did not even so much as scream. Instead, in a flash she had the ropes off the carrying pole and, holding the pole slantwise across her body, took up a posture of defense.

Even Yasuo had to admit he must have been a sorry sight in Hatsue's eyes. She retreated a step or two before him, keeping the same defensive posture.

Yasuo decided it would be better to turn it all off as a joke. He broke into foolish laughter and said:

"Hey! I guess I scared you. You thought I was a hobgoblin, didn't you?"

"Why, it's Brother Yasuo!"

"I thought I'd hide here and give you a scare."

"But—at this time of night?"

The girl did not yet realize how very attractive she was. Perhaps she might have if she had thought about it deeply enough, but just now she accepted Yasuo's explanation that he had actually hidden here for no other reason than to frighten her.

In an instant, taking advantage of her trustfulness, Yasuo snatched the pole away from her and caught her by the right wrist. The leather of Yasuo's jacket was making creaking sounds.

Yasuo had finally recovered his poise. He stood glaring at Hatsue. Now he was quite self-possessed and, intending to win the girl fairly, he fell unconsciously into an imitation of the open and aboveboard manner he imagined Shinji must have used on a similar occasion.

"All right," he said reasonably, "now will you listen to what I've got to say? You'll be sorry if you don't. So you'd better listen—unless you want everybody to know about you and Shinji."

Hatsue's face was flushed and she was breathing hard.

"Let go of my arm! What do you mean—about me and Shinji?"

"Don't act so innocent. As though you haven't been playing around with Shinji! You really put one over on me."

"Don't say such ridiculous things. I haven't done any such thing."

"Me, I know all about it. What was it you did with Shinji up on the mountain the other day in the storm? . . . Hey! just look at her blush! . . . So now you're going to do the same thing with me. Come on! Come on!"

"Get away! Get away from me!" Hatsue struggled, trying to escape.

Yasuo would not let her go. She would be sure to tell her father if she got away now before anything happened. But afterwards—then she wouldn't tell a soul. Yasuo was hopelessly addicted to the pulp magazines, which came from the city, with their frequent confessions of girls who had been "seduced." What a grand feeling it was to be able to do this to a girl and yet be sure that she could never tell anyone about it!

Yasuo finally had Hatsue pinned to the ground beside the spring. One of the buckets had been knocked over and the water was running over the moss-covered earth. The light of the street lamp showed Hatsue's nostrils quivering and her wide-open eyes flashing. Her hair was half in the spilled water.

Suddenly Hatsue pursed her lips and spat full on Yasuo's chin.

This aroused his passion all the more and, feeling her heaving breasts beneath him, he thrust his face against her cheek.

At that moment he gave a shout and jumped to his feet: the hornet had stung him again, this time on the nape of the neck.

Angered beyond endurance, he tried wildly to catch the hornet, and while he was dancing about, Hatsue went running toward the stone steps.

Yasuo was in a panic of confusion. He was fully occupied with the hornet, and yet still managed somehow to satisfy his urge to recapture Hatsue, but from one moment to the next he had no idea which action he was performing, nor in what order. At any rate, catch Hatsue again he did.

No sooner had he forced her ripening body down again onto the moss than the persistent hornet lit, this time on the seat of Yasuo's trousers, and drove its stinger deeply into the flesh of a buttock.

Hatsue was gaining experience in the art of escape and, when Yasuo leaped up, this time she fled to the far side of the spring. As she dived into the grove of trees and ran to hide behind a clump of ferns, she caught sight of a big rock. Holding the rock over her head in both hands, she finally got her breath and looked down across the spring.

As a matter of fact, until that moment Hatsue had not known what god it was who had come to her rescue. But now, as she suspiciously watched Yasuo's mad cavortings on the other side of the spring, she realized it was all the doing of a clever hornet. Yasuo's hands clawed the air and she could see, just at their fingertips, full in the light of the street lamp, the flashing of little, golden-colored wings.

When he at last realized he had driven the hornet away, Yasuo stood looking blank and wiped the sweat off his face with his handcloth. Then he looked around for Hatsue. Seeing no trace of her, he made a trumpet with his hands and nervously called her name in a low voice.

Hatsue deliberately rustled some ferns with her toe.

"Come on down from up there, won't you? I promise not to do anything else."

"No, I won't."

"Come on down—please."

He started to climb up, and Hatsue brandished the stone. Yasuo drew back.

"Hey, what're you doing! Watch out—that's dangerous. . . . What can I do to get you to come down?"

Yasuo would have liked to run away without more ceremony, but his fear that she would tell her father kept him wheedling:

". . . Please! I'll do anything you say, just so you come on down. . . . I suppose you're going to tell your father on me, aren't you?"

There was no answer.

"Come on, please don't tell your father? I'll do any-

thing you say if only you won't tell. . . . What do you
want me to do?"

"Well, if you'll draw the water for me and carry it all
the way home . . ."

"Really?"

"Really."

"All right, I'll sure do it then. That Uncle Teru is really
something to be afraid of!"

Then Yasuo silently set about his task—earnestly, whole-
heartedly, making a truly ridiculous sight. He refilled the
bucket that had been overturned, put the rope handles
of the buckets on the pole, shouldered the pole, and began
walking. . . .

After a moment Yasuo glanced back and saw that Hatsue had come down from the grove without his knowing
it and was following along about two yards behind him.
She did not so much as smile. When she saw him stop
walking, she stopped too, and when he started on down
the steps again, she started too.

The village was still buried in sleep, its roofs bathed in
moonlight. But as they descended the stone stairs toward
the village, step by step, they could hear rising up to them
the crowing of cocks from all sides, a sign that the dawn
was near.

# 10

SHINJI'S BROTHER returned home to the island. The mothers were waiting on the jetty to welcome their sons. There was a drizzling rain and the open sea was invisible. The ferryboat was only about a hundred yards from the jetty when its shape came into view through the mist.

In the same breath each mother called the name of her own son. Now they could plainly see the caps and handkerchiefs being waved from the deck.

The boat had arrived, but even when they were ashore, face to face with their mothers, these middle-school boys only smiled a little and went right on playing around among themselves. They all disliked showing affection for their mothers in each other's presence.

Even after he was at his own home, Hiroshi was still too excited to settle down. About all he could tell of his trip were incidents such as the morning he had been so sleepy because one of his friends had been afraid to go to the toilet by himself the night before and had pounded Hiroshi awake in the middle of the night to go with him. But not a word did Hiroshi have for all the famous historic spots they had visited.

Certainly Hiroshi had brought back some deep impressions from his trip, but he did not know how to put them into words. He would try to think of something to say, and all he could recall would be something like the time, already a year or so ago, when he had had such fun waxing a spot on the corridor floor at school and seeing one of the women teachers slip on it and fall. Those gleaming streetcars and automobiles that had come upon him so suddenly, flashed by, and disappeared, those towering buildings and neon lights that had so amazed him—where were they now?

Here at home, looking just the same as they had before he had gone away, there were still the same old cupboard, wall clock, Buddhist altar, dining-table, dressing-table—and the same old mother. There were the cook-stove and the dirty straw mats. These things could understand him even without words. And yet all of them, including even his mother, were at him to tell them about his travels.

Hiroshi finally calmed down about the time Shinji came home from the day's fishing. After supper he opened his travel diary and gave his mother and brother a perfunctory account of his trip. Satisfied, they ceased questioning him about the excursion.

Everything was back to normal. His became again an existence in which everything was understood without the need for words. The cupboard, the wall clock, his mother, his brother, the old sooty cookstove, the sea's roaring . . . folded in these familiar arms, Hiroshi slept soundly.

Hiroshi's summer vacation was nearing its end. So every day from the moment he got up until he went to bed he was playing with all his might.

The island abounded in places to play. Hiroshi and his friends had finally seen the Western movies that until that time they had only heard about, and the new game of cowboys and Indians had now become a great favorite with them. The sight of smoke rising from a forest fire around Motoura, on Shima Peninsula across the sea, inevitably reminded them of signal fires rising from some Indian stronghold.

The cormorants of Uta-jima were birds of passage, and by this time of year they were vanishing one by one. All over the island the songs of nightingales were now frequently heard. The steep pass leading down to the middle school was known as Red Nose Pass because of its effect on the noses of passers-by in the winter, when it received every blast that blew, but now, no matter how cool the day, the breezes there would not even so much as turn a nose pink.

Benten Promontory, at the southern tip of the island, provided the boys with their Western locale. The western side of the promontory was entirely of limestone, and it led finally to the entrance of a cave, one of the most mysterious spots on Uta-jima.

The entrance to the cave was small, only about a yard and a half wide and two feet high, but the winding passageway leading into the interior gradually widened out into a three-tiered cavern. Until that point the passageway was truly black, but a strange half-light wavered within the cavern proper. This was because the cave actually went completely through the promontory to an invisible opening on the eastern side, where the sea entered, rising and falling at the bottom of a deep shaft in the rock.

Candles in hand, the gang entered the cave. Calling "Watch out!" and "Be careful!" to each other, they went crawling through the dark passageway. They could see each other's faces floating on the darkness, tinted with grimness in the flickering candlelight, and they thought how wonderful they would look in this light if only they had the unshaven beards of young toughs.

The gang was made up of Hiroshi, Sochan, and Katchan. They were on their way to search for Indian treasure deep in the farthest recesses of the cavern. Sochan was in the lead, and when they came out into the cavern, where they could at last stand erect, his head was splendidly covered with thickly woven cobwebs.

"Hey! look at you!" Hiroshi and Katchan chorused. "Your hair's all decorated. You can be the chieftain."

They stood their three candles up beneath a Sanskrit inscription some unknown person had carved long ago on one of the moss-covered walls.

The sea, ebbing and flowing in the shaft at the eastern end of the cave, roared fiercely as it dashed against the rocks. The sound of the surging waves was completely different from that to which they were accustomed outside. It was a seething sound that echoed off the limestone walls of the cavern, the reverberations overlapping each other until the entire cave was aroar and seemed to be pitching and swaying. Shudderingly they recalled the legend that between the sixteenth and eighteenth days of the sixth moon seven pure-white sharks were supposed to appear out of nowhere within that shaft to the sea.

In this game the boys changed their parts at will, shifting between the roles of enemies and friends with the greatest of ease. Sochan had been made an Indian chief because of the cobwebs in his hair, and the other two were frontier guards, implacable enemies of all Indians, but now, wanting to ask the chief why the waves echoed so frighteningly, they suddenly became his two loyal braves.

Sochan understood the change immediately and seated himself with great dignity on a rock beneath the candles.

"O Chief, what terrible sound is this that we hear?"

"This, my children," said Sochan in solemn tones, "this is the god showing his anger."

"And what can we do to appease the god's anger?" Hiroshi asked.

"Well, now, let me see. . . . Yes, the only thing to do is to make him an offering and then pray."

So they took the rice crackers and bean-jam buns that they had either received or filched from their mothers, arranged them on a sheet of newspaper, and ceremonially placed them on a rock overlooking the shaft.

Chief Sochan walked between the two braves, advancing with pomp to the altar, where after prostrating himself on the limestone floor he raised both arms high, chanted a curious, impromptu incantation, and then prayed, bending the upper half of his body back and forth. Behind the chieftain Hiroshi and Katchan went through the same genuflections. The cold surface of the stone pressed through their trousers and touched their kneecaps, and all the while Hiroshi and the others felt themselves in very truth to be characters in a movie.

Fortunately, the god's wrath seemed to have been placated, and the roar of the waves became a little quieter. So they sat in a circle and ate the offerings of rice crackers and bean-jam buns from the altar. The food tasted ten times more delicious than usual.

Just then a still more tremendous roar sounded, and a spray of water flung itself high out of the shaft. In the gloom the sudden spray looked like a white phantom; the waters set the cavern to rumbling and swaying; and it seemed as though the sea were looking for a chance to snatch even these three Indians, seated in a circle within the stone room, and pull them to its depths.

In spite of themselves, Hiroshi, Sochan, and Katchan were afraid, and when a stray gust of wind blew out of nowhere, fluttering the flames of the candles beneath the Sanskrit inscription and finally blowing one out altogether, their fear grew still stronger. But the three of them were always trying to outdo each other in displays of bravery; so, with the cheerful instinct of all boys, they quickly hid their fear under the guise of playing the game.

Hiroshi and Katchan became two cowardly Indian braves, trembling with fear.

"Oh! oh! I'm afraid! I'm afraid! O Chief, the god is terribly angry. What could have made him so angry? Tell us, O Chief."

Sochan sat on a throne of stone, trembling and shaking majestically like the chieftain he was. Pressed for an answer, he recalled the gossip that had been secretly whispered about the island during the past few days and, without any evil purpose, decided to make use of it. He cleared his throat and spoke:

"It is because of an immorality. It is because of an unrighteousness."

"Immorality?" asked Hiroshi. "What do you mean?"

"Don't you know, Hiroshi? I mean what your brother Shinji did to Miyata's daughter Hatsue—I mean *omeko*—that's what. And that's what the god is angry about."

Hearing his brother mentioned and feeling something disgraceful was being said about him, Hiroshi flared out at the chieftain in a rage:

"What's that you say my brother did with Sister Hatsue? What do you mean by *omeko*?"

"Don't you even know that? It means when a boy and a girl sleep together!"

Actually, Sochan himself knew little more about the word than this. But he knew how to smear his explanation thoroughly with insulting colors, and in a fit of rage Hiroshi went flying at Sochan.

Before he realized it, Sochan felt his shoulders grabbed and his cheek slapped. But the scuffle ended disappointingly soon: when Sochan was knocked against the wall the two remaining candles fell to the ground and went out.

In the cavern there remained only the dim light, barely sufficient for them to see each other's faces vaguely. Hiroshi and Sochan were still facing each other, breathing hard, but they gradually realized what danger they were inviting by fighting in such a spot.

Katchan intervened, saying:

"Stop fighting! Can't you see it's dangerous here?"

So they struck matches, found their candles, and went crawling out of the cave, saying practically nothing. . . .

By the time they had scrambled up the cliff, bathed in the bright light of outdoors, and reached the ridge of the promontory, they were again as good friends as ever, seeming to have forgotten all about their fight of a little while before. They walked the narrow path along the ridge of the promontory singing:

*Along the Five League Beach of Benten-Hachijo,*
*And all along the Garden Beach . . .*

This Five League Beach was the most beautiful stretch of coastline on the island, lying along the western side of Benten Promontory. Halfway along the beach towered a huge rock called Hachijo Isle, as tall as a two-storied house, and, just now, among the rank-growing vines on its summit, there were four or five playful urchins, waving their hands and shouting something.

The three boys waved back in reply and walked on along the path. Here and there in the soft grass among the pine trees there were patches of milk vetch blooming red.

"Look! the seining boats!" Katchan pointed to the sea off the eastern shore of the promontory.

On that shore the Garden Beach embraced a lovely little cove, and at its mouth there were now three seining boats floating motionless, waiting for the tide. These were the boats that manipulated the drag-nets as they were pulled along the ocean floor by larger vessels.

Hiroshi said "Look!" also and, together with his friends, squinted out over the dazzling sea, but the words Sochan had spoken earlier still weighed on his spirit, seeming to become heavier and heavier as time passed.

At suppertime Hiroshi returned home with an empty stomach. Shinji was not yet home and his mother was alone, feeding brushwood into the cookstove. There was the sound of the crackling wood and the windlike sound of the fire inside the stove, and it was only at times like this that delicious smells erased the stench of the toilet.

"Mother," Hiroshi said, lying spread-eagled on the straw matting.

"What?"

"What's *omeko?* Somebody said that's what Shinji did to Hatsue. What'd they mean?"

Before Hiroshi realized it, his mother had left the stove and was sitting straight beside the spot where he lay. Her eyes were flashing strangely, flashing through some fallen strands of hair to give her a frightening look.

"Hiroshi—you—where'd you hear that? Who said such a thing?"

"Sochan."

"Don't you ever say that again! You mustn't even say that to your brother. If you do, it'll be many a day before I give you anything to eat again. Do you hear what I say?"

The mother took a very tolerant view of young people's amorous affairs. And even during the diving season, when everyone stood about the drying-fire gossiping, she held her tongue. But when it came to its being her own son's affair that was the subject of malicious gossip, then there was a motherly duty that she would have to perform.

That night, after Hiroshi was asleep, the mother leaned close to Shinji's ear and spoke in a low, firm voice:

"Do you know people are spreading bad stories about you and Hatsue?"

Shinji shook his head and blushed. His mother too was embarrassed, but she pressed the point with unwavering frankness.

"Did you sleep with her?"

Again Shinji shook his head.

"Then you've not done a thing that people could talk about? Are you telling me the truth?"

"Yes, I've told you the truth."

"All right, then there's nothing for me to say. But do be careful—people are always minding other people's business."

But the situation did not take a turn for the better. The following evening Shinji's mother went to a meeting of the Ape-god Society, the women's one and only club, and, the moment she appeared, everyone stopped talking, looking as though they had just had a wet blanket thrown over them. Obviously they had been gossiping.

The next evening, when Shinji went to the Young Men's Association, flinging the door open as casually as always, he found a group of youths gathered around the desk, eagerly discussing something beneath the glare of the unshaded electric bulb. When they caught sight of Shinji they fell silent for a moment. There was nothing but the sound of the sea floating in to fill the bleak room, seemingly empty of all human life.

As usual, Shinji sat down against the wall, wrapped his arms around his knees, and said not a word. Thereupon everyone began talking again in their usual noisy way, about a different subject, and Yasuo, the president, who had come to the meeting strangely early today, greeted Shinji from across the desk in a hail-fellow-well-met way. Shinji returned the greeting with an unsuspecting smile.

A few days later, while they were eating their lunch on the *Taihei-maru* and resting from fishing, Ryuji spoke up as though unable to contain himself any longer:

"Brother Shin, it really makes my blood boil—the way

Yasuo is going around saying such bad things about you—"

"Is he?" Shinji smiled and kept a manly silence.

The boat was gently rolling on the spring waves.

Suddenly Jukichi, usually so taciturn, broke into the conversation:

"I know. I know. That Yasuo is jealous. The scamp's nothing but a big fool, sticking up his nose because of his father. He makes me sick. So now Shinji too has become a great ladies' man and Yasuo's burned up with jealousy. Don't you pay any attention to what they say, Shinji. If there's any trouble, I'm on your side."

Thus the rumor which Chiyoko had originated and Yasuo had broadcast came to be whispered persistently at every crossroads in the village. And yet it still had not reached the ears of Hatsue's father. Then one night there occurred the incident that the village would not tire of talking about for months to come. It took place at the public bathhouse.

Even the richest houses in the village did not have their own baths, and on this night Terukichi Miyata went to the public bath as usual. He brushed through the curtain at the entrance with a haughty toss of the head, ripped off his clothes as though plucking a fowl, and flung them toward a wicker basket. His singlet and sash missed the basket and scattered themselves across the floor. Clicking his tongue loudly, he picked the garments up with his toes and threw them in the basket. It was an awesome sight to those who were watching, but this was one of the few opportunities left for Hatsue's father to give public proof that, old though he was, his vigor was undiminished.

Actually, his aged nudity was a marvel to behold. His gold-and-copper-colored limbs showed no sign of slackness, and above his piercing eyes and stubborn forehead his white hair bristled wildly like the mane of a lion. His chest was a ruddy red from many years of heavy drinking, providing an impressive contrast for his white hair. His bulging muscles had become hardened through long disuse, reinforcing the impression of a crag that has become all the more precipitous under the pounding of the waves.

It might be better to say that Terukichi was the personification of all Uta-jima's toil and determination and ambition and strength. Full of the somewhat uncouth energy of a man who had raised his family from nothing to wealth in a single generation, he was also narrow-minded enough never to have accepted any public office in the village, a fact that made him all the more respected by the leading people of the village. The uncanny accuracy of his weather predictions, his matchless experience in matters of fishing and navigation, and the great pride he took in knowing all the history and traditions of the island were often offset by his uncompromising stubbornness, his ludicrous pretensions, and his pugnacity, which abated not a whit with the years. But in any case he was an old man who, while still living, could act like a bronze statue erected to his own memory—and without appearing ridiculous.

He slid open the glass door leading from the dressing-room into the bath.

The bathroom was fairly crowded, and through the clouds of steam there appeared the vague outlines of people moving about. The ceiling resounded with the sounds of water, the light tapping noises of wooden basins, and laughing conversation; the room was filled with abundant hot water and a feeling of release after the day's labor.

Terukichi never rinsed his body before entering the pool. Now as always he walked in long, dignified strides directly from the door to the pool and, without further ado, thrust his legs into the water. It made no difference to him how hot the water might be. Terukichi had no more interest in such things as the possible effect of heat upon his heart and the blood vessels in his brain than he had in, say, perfume or neckties.

Even though their faces got splashed with water, when the bathers realized it was Terukichi they nodded to him courteously. Terukichi immersed himself up to his arrogant chin.

There were two young fishermen who were washing themselves beside the pool and had not noticed Terukichi's arrival. In loud voices they went right on with their unrestrained gossip about Terukichi.

"Uncle Teru Miyata really must be in his second childhood. He doesn't even know his girl's become a cracked pitcher."

"That Shinji Kubo—didn't he pull a fast one though? While everybody was thinking he was such a kid, there he went and stole her right from under Uncle Teru's nose."

The people in the pool were fidgety and kept their eyes turned away from Terukichi.

Terukichi was boiling red, but his face was outwardly composed as he got out of the pool. Taking a wooden basin in each hand, he went and filled them from the cold-water tank. Then he walked over to the two youths, poured the icy water over their heads without warning, and kicked them in the back.

The boys, their eyes half closed with soap, immediately started to strike back. But then they realized it was Teru-kichi they were up against and hesitated.

The old man next caught them both by the scruff of the neck, and, even though their soapy skin was slippery under his fingers, dragged them to the edge of the pool. There he gave them a tremendous shove, burying their heads in the hot water. Still grasping their necks tightly in his big hands, the old man shook the two heads in the water and knocked them together, just as though he were rinsing out laundry.

Then, to top it all, without even washing himself, Teru-kichi stalked from the room with his long strides, not giving so much as a glance at the backsides of the other bath-ers, who had now risen to their feet and were left staring after him in blank amazement.

WHILE THEY WERE EATING their lunch the next day on
the *Taihei-maru,* the master opened his tobacco pouch
and took out a piece of paper folded very small. Grinning
broadly, he held it out to Shinji. But when Shinji reached
for it, Jukichi said:

"Now listen—if I give you this, will you promise not to
start loafing around after you've read it?"

"I'm not that sort of fellow," Shinji replied definitely
and to the point.

"All right, it's a man's promise. . . . This morning
when I was passing Uncle Teru's house, Hatsue came
trotting out and pressed this note tight in my hand. She
didn't say a word and went right back inside. I was tickled
to think of getting a love letter at my age, but then I
opened it, and how should it begin but 'Dear Shinji'! 'You

109

old fool,' I told myself, and I was just about to tear it up and throw it in the ocean. But then I told myself that would be a shame, so I brought it along for you."

Shinji took the note, while both the master and Ryuji laughed.

The thin paper had been folded many times into a small pellet, and Shinji opened it gingerly, careful not to tear it in his thick, knobby fingers. Tobacco dust sifted onto his hands from the folds. She had started writing on the notepaper with ink, but after a few lines her fountain pen had apparently run dry and she had continued with a faint pencil. Written in a childish hand, the note said:

"*. . . Last night at the bath Father heard some very bad gossip about us and became terribly angry and commanded that I must never see Shinji-san again. No matter how much I explained, it was no use, not with Father's being the kind of man he is. He says I must never go out of the house from the time the fishing-boats come back in the afternoon until after they've gone out in the morning. He says he'll get the lady next door to draw water for us when our turn comes. So there's nothing I can do. I'm so miserable, so very miserable I can't stand it. And he says that on the days when the boats don't go out he'll be right at my side and never take his eyes off me.*

"*How will I ever be able to see Shinji-san again? Please think of some way for us to meet. I'm afraid for us to send letters by mail because the old postmaster would know all about it. So every day I'll write a letter and stick it under the lid on the water jar in front of our kitchen. Please put your replies the same place. But it would be dangerous for you to come here yourself to get the letters, so please get some friend you trust to come for you. I've been on the*

*island such a short time that I don't know anybody I can
really trust.*

"*Oh, Shinji-san, let us go on truly, with strong hearts!
Every day I will be praying before the memorial tablets of
my mother and brother that no accident will befall Shinji-
san. I'm sure that they in heaven will understand how I
feel.*"

As Shinji read the note the expression on his face alternated, like sunshine and shadow, between the sorrow of
being separated from Hatsue and the joy of having this
proof of her affection for him.

Just as Shinji finished reading the note, Jukichi
snatched it out of his hands, as though this were only
the rightful due of a bearer of love messages, and read it
through. Not only did he read it aloud for Ryuji's benefit,
but he also read it in his own unique, ballad-chanting
style. Shinji knew that Jukichi always read the newspaper
aloud to himself in this same chanting tone and that he
was using it now without the slightest malice, but still
it hurt to have such a travesty made of those earnest
words, written by the girl he loved.

As a matter of fact, Jukichi was sincerely moved by
the letter and, during the reading, he heaved many a big
sigh and threw in many an interjection. When he was
done he gave his opinion in the same powerful voice he
used to give fishing orders, a voice that now boomed out
over the quiet noonday sea to a radius of a hundred yards
in all directions:

"Women really are wise ones, aren't they?"

Here in the boat there were none to hear except these
two whom he trusted, so at Jukichi's urging Shinji gradually confided in them. His way of telling the story was

awkward. Events were often told in the wrong order, and
he would leave out important points. It took him quite
a time just to give a brief outline. Finally he reached the
heart of the matter and told them how on that day of
the storm, even though they were naked in each other's
arms, he had been unable to win the prize after all.

At this point Jukichi, who almost never smiled, could
not stop laughing.

"If it'd been me! Oh, if it'd been me! Really, what a
mess you made of things. But then I guess that's what
comes of your being such a virgin. And, besides, the
girl's so almighty strait-laced that she was too big a
handful for you. But still it's a ridiculous story. . . . Oh,
well, it'll be all right after she's your wife; then you'll
make up for it by giving her the rod ten times a day."

Ryuji, a year younger than Shinji, was listening to this
talk as though he only half understood it. As for Shinji,
he was not sensitive and easily wounded the way a city-
bred boy is during the time of his first love, and to Shinji
the old man's raillery was actually soothing and comfort-
ing rather than upsetting. The gentle waves that rocked
their boat also calmed his heart, and now that he had
told the whole story he was at peace; this place of toil
had become for him a place of matchless rest.

Ryuji, who passed Terukichi's house on his way to the
beach, volunteered to pick up Hatsue's letter from under
the lid of the water jar each morning.

"So from tomorrow you'll be the new postmaster,"
said Jukichi, making one of his rare jokes.

The daily letters became the principal subject of conversation during their lunch hours on the boat, and the
three of them always shared the anguish and the anger

called forth by the contents of the letters. The second letter in particular aroused their indignation. In it Hatsue described at length how Yasuo had attacked her by the spring in the middle of the night and the threats he'd made. She'd kept her promise and not told about it, but Yasuo had avenged himself by spreading that false story about her and Shinji through the village. Then, when her father had forbidden her to see Shinji again, she had explained everything honestly and had also told him of Yasuo's disgraceful behavior, but her father had not done a thing about Yasuo, had, in fact, even remained on as friendly terms as ever with Yasuo's family, with the same visiting back and forth. But she herself detested the very sight of Yasuo's face. She ended the letter by assuring Shinji that she would never, never let her guard down against Yasuo.

Ryuji became excited on Shinji's behalf, and even Shinji's eyes flashed with a rare expression of anger.

"It's all because I'm poor," Shinji said.

He was usually not one to let such querulous words pass his lips. And he felt tears of shame springing in his eyes, not because he was poor, but because he had been weak enough to give voice to such a complaint. But then he tightened his face with all his might, defying those unexpected tears, and managed to avoid the double shame of having the others see him cry.

This time Jukichi did not laugh.

Jukichi took great pleasure in tobacco and had the odd habit of alternating between a pipe one day and cigarettes the next. Today was the turn for cigarettes. On pipe days he was forever knocking his tiny, old-fashioned brass pipe against the side of the boat, a habit that had worn a small trough in a certain spot on the gunwale. It was because he prized his ship so greatly that he had decided to forgo his pipe every other day and smoke New Life cigarettes instead, carving himself a coral holder for the purpose.

Jukichi turned his eyes away from the two youths and, the coral holder clamped between his teeth, gazed out over the misty expanse of the Gulf of Ise. Cape Moro, at the tip of Chita Peninsula, was faintly visible through the mist.

Jukichi Oyama's face was like leather. The sun had burned it almost black down to the very bottom of its deep wrinkles, and it gleamed like polished leather. His eyes were sharp and full of life, but they had lost the clarity of youth and, in its place, seemed to have been glazed with the same tough dirt that coated his skin, making them able to withstand any light, no matter how brilliant.

Because of his age and his great experience as a fisherman he knew how to wait tranquilly. Now he said:

"I know exactly what you two are thinking. You're planning to give Yasuo a beating. But you listen to me—that won't do a bit of good. A fool's a fool, so just leave him alone. Guess it's hard for Shinji, but patience is the main thing. That's what it takes to catch a fish. Everything's going to be all right now for sure. Right's sure to win, even if it doesn't say anything. Uncle Teru's no fool, and don't you ever think he can't tell a fresh fish from a rotten one. Just you leave Yasuo alone. Right's sure to win in the end."

Even though it was always a day late, village gossip reached the lighthouse together with the daily deliveries of mail and food. And the news that Terukichi had forbidden Hatsue to see Shinji turned Chiyoko's heart black with feelings of guilt. She comforted herself with the thought that Shinji did not know she was the source of this false gossip. But, even so, she simply could not look Shinji in the eye when he came one day to bring fish, completely cast down in spirits. And on the other hand her good-natured parents, not knowing the reason, were worried over Chiyoko's moroseness.

Chiyoko's spring vacation was drawing to a close and the day came when she was to return to her dormitory in Tokyo. She simply could not bring herself to confess what she had done, and yet she had the feeling that she could not return to Tokyo until she asked Shinji to forgive her. If she did not confess her guilt, there was no particular reason for Shinji to be angry with her, but still she wanted to beg his pardon.

So she got herself invited to spend the night before her departure for Tokyo at the house of the postmaster in the village, and before dawn the next morning she went out alone.

The beach was already busy with preparations for the day's fishing, and people were going about their work in the starlight. The boats, pulled on the "abacus" frames and urged on by many shouting voices, inched reluctantly down toward the water's edge. Nothing could be seen distinctly except the white of the towels and sweat cloths the men had tied around their heads.

Step by step, Chiyoko's wooden clogs sank into the cold sand. And in its turn the sand slithered whisperingly off the arches of her feet.

Everyone was busy and no one looked at Chiyoko. She realized with a pang of shame that here all these people were, caught fast in the monotonous but powerful whirlpool of earning a daily living, burning out the very depths of their bodies and souls, and that not one of them was the sort of person who could become engrossed in sentimental problems such as hers.

Nevertheless Chiyoko peered eagerly through the dawn's darkness, looking for Shinji. All the men were dressed alike and it was difficult to distinguish their faces in the morning twilight.

One boat finally hit the waves and floated on the water as though it had been freed from cramped confinement. Instinctively Chiyoko moved toward it and then called out to a young man with a white towel tied around his head.

The youth had been about to jump aboard, but now he stopped and turned back. His smiling face revealed the whiteness of two clean rows of teeth, and Chiyoko knew for certain it was Shinji.

"I'm leaving today. I wanted to say good-by."

"Oh, you're leaving? . . ." Shinji fell silent, and then in an unnatural tone of voice, as though he were trying to decide what would be best to say, he added:

"Well . . . good-by."

Shinji was in a hurry. Realizing this, Chiyoko felt even more hurried than he. No words would come, much less a confession. She closed her eyes, praying that Shinji would stay before her even one second more. In this moment she realized that her wanting to beg his pardon was actually nothing but a mask to conceal her long-felt desire to have him be kind to her.

What was it she was wanting to be forgiven for, this girl who was so convinced of her ugliness? On the spur of the moment, without thought, she let slip the question she had always kept pushed down in the very bottom of her heart, a question she probably could never have asked anyone but this one boy:

"Shinji—am I so ugly?"

"What?" the boy asked, a puzzled look on his face.

"My face—is it so ugly?"

Chiyoko hoped the dawn's darkness would protect her face, making her appear even the slightest bit beautiful. But the sea to the east—didn't it seem to be already turning light?

Shinji's answer was immediate. Being in a hurry, he escaped a situation in which too slow an answer would have cut into the girl's heart.

"What makes you say that? You're pretty," he said, one hand on the stern and one foot already beginning the leap that would carry him into the boat. "You're pretty."

As everyone well knew, Shinji was incapable of flattery. Now, pressed for time, he had simply given a felicitous answer to her urgent question.

The boat began to move. He waved back to her cheerfully from the boat as it pulled away.

And it was a happy girl who was left standing at the water's edge.

Later that morning her parents came down from the lighthouse to see her off, and even while she talked with them Chiyoko's face was full of life. They were surprised to see how happy their daughter was to be returning to Tokyo.

The *Kamikaze-maru* pulled away from the jetty, and Chiyoko was finally alone on the warm deck. In the solitude her feeling of happiness, on which she had been pondering constantly all morning, became complete.

"He said I'm pretty! He said I'm pretty!" Chiyoko repeated yet again the refrain she had said over and over to herself how many hundreds of times since that moment.

"That's really what he said. And that's enough for me. I mustn't expect more than that. That's really what he said to me. I must be satisfied with that and not expect him to love me too. He—he has someone else to love. . . . What a wicked thing it was I did to him! What terrible unhappiness my jealousy has caused him! And yet he repaid my wickedness by saying I'm pretty. I must make it up to him . . . somehow I must do whatever I can to return his kindness. . . ."

Chiyoko's reveries were broken by a strange sound of singing that drifted across the waves. When she looked she saw a fleet of boats, covered with red banners, sailing from the direction of the Irako Channel.

"What are those?" Chiyoko asked the captain's young assistant, who was coiling a hawser on the deck.

"They're pilgrim boats bound for the Ise Shrines. The fishermen from around Enshu and Yaizu on Suruga Bay bring their families with them on the bonito boats to Toba. All those red flags have the boats' names on them. They have a great time drinking and singing and gambling all the way."

The red banners became more and more distinct, and as the fast, ocean-going fishing-boats drew near the *Kamikaze-maru*, the singing voices borne on the wind were almost raucous.

Once more Chiyoko repeated to herself:

"He told me I'm pretty."

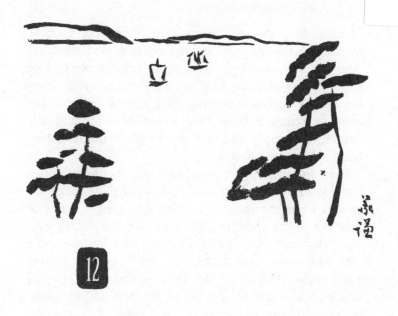

## 12

In this way the spring had neared its end. It was still too early for the clusters of crinum lilies that bloomed in the cliffs on the eastern side of the island, but the fields were colored here and there with various other flowers. The children were back in school again, and some of the women were already diving in the cold water for the seaweed called "soft lace." As a consequence there were now more houses that were empty during the daytime, doors unlocked, windows open. Bees entered these empty houses freely, flew about in them lonesomely, and were often startled upon running headlong into a mirror.

Shinji, not clever at scheming, had been able to discover no way to meet Hatsue. Although their meetings before had been few and far between, still the happy anticipation of their next meeting had made the waiting bearable. But now that he knew there could be no next meeting, his longing to see her became even stronger. And yet the promise he had given Jukichi not to loaf made it impossible for him to take even a day off from fishing. So there was nothing for him to do every night after he returned from fishing but to wait until the streets were empty and then prowl about the neighborhood of Hatsue's house.

Sometimes an upstairs window would be thrown open and Hatsue would look out. Except on those lucky occasions when the moon was shining just right, her face was lost in the shadows. Even so, the boy's sharp eyesight allowed him to see clearly even how her eyes were wet with tears. Out of fear of the neighbors Hatsue never spoke. And Shinji too, from behind the stone wall of the small vegetable garden at the back of her house, would simply stand looking up at the girl's face, not saying a word. Without fail, the letter Ryuji would bring the next day would dwell at great length upon the pain of such an ephemeral meeting, and as Shinji read the words Hatsue's image and voice would finally come into focus together, and in his mind the wordless girl he had seen the night before would come alive with speech and action.

Such meetings were painful for Shinji too, and there were times when he preferred to relieve his pent-up emotions by wandering to those parts of the island where people seldom came. Sometimes he went as far as the ancient burial mound of Prince Deki. The exact boundaries of the tumulus were not clear, but at the highest point there were seven ancient pine trees and, in the midst of them, a small *torii* and shrine.

. . .

The legend of Prince Deki was vague. Nothing was known even about the origins of his strange name. In a time-honored ceremony held during the lunar New Year, the strange box that reposed in the shrine was briefly opened each year and old couples of more than sixty years of age were allowed a fleeting glimpse of the object it contained, which looked like an ancient nobleman's fan-shaped baton, but no one knew what relationship there was between this mysterious treasure and Prince Deki. Until about a generation past the children of the island had called their mothers *eya,* and this was said to have arisen from the fact that the prince had called his wife *heya* meaning "room," and that his infant heir had mis-pronounced the word as *eya* when trying to imitate his father.

Be that as it may, the story goes that long, long ago, in a golden ship, the prince drifted from a far land to this island, took a girl of the island to wife, and when he died was buried in an imperial tumulus. No accounts have been handed down concerning the prince's life, nor are there recounted any of those tragic tales that are apt to grow up and adhere to such a legendary figure. Assuming the legend to be based on fact, this silence suggests that Prince Deki's life on Uta-jima must have been so happy and uneventful that it left no room for the birth of tragic yarns.

Perhaps Prince Deki was a heavenly being who descended to a nameless land. Perhaps he lived out his earthly years without being recognized and, do what he would, will as he could, was never separated from happiness, nor from the blessings of Heaven. Perhaps this is

121

the reason why his remains were interred in a mound over-looking the beautiful Five League Beach and Hachijo Isle, leaving behind not a single story. . . .

But the boy knew only unhappiness as he wandered about the shrine until exhausted. Then he sat down absent-mindedly on the grass, hugged his knees, and gazed out at the moonlit sea. There was a halo around the moon, foretelling rain on the morrow. . . .

The next morning when Ryuji stopped by Hatsue's house to pick up the daily letter, he found it sticking out a little from under one corner of the wooden lid on the water jar, covered with a metal basin to keep the rain from wetting it.

The rain continued during the entire day's fishing, but Shinji managed to read the letter during the noon rest by protecting it with his raincoat.

Her handwriting was terribly difficult to read, and she explained that she was writing in her bed early in the morning, groping in the dark to avoid arousing her father's suspicions by turning on the light. Usually she wrote her letters at odd moments during the day and "posted" them before the fishing-boats went out the next morning, but this morning, she wrote, she had something she wanted to tell him at once, so she had torn up the long letter she had written him yesterday and was writing this in its place.

Hatsue's letter went on to say that she had had a lucky dream. In the dream a god had told her that Shinji was a reincarnation of Prince Deki. Then they had been happily married and had had a jewel-like child.

Shinji knew that Hatsue could not have known about his visit to Prince Deki's tomb the night before. He was so struck by this uncanny happening that he decided to write Hatsue at length when he got home that night and tell her this amazing proof of her dream's deep meaning.

Now that Shinji was working to support the family it was no longer necessary for his mother to go diving when the water was still cold. So she had decided to wait until June to start diving. But she had always been a hard worker, and now, as the weather became warm, she became dissatisfied, with nothing to do but the housework. Whenever she found herself unoccupied she was apt to let herself become upset with all sorts of unnecessary worries.

Her son's unhappiness was always on her mind. Shinji was now completely different from the person he had been three months before. He was as taciturn as ever, but the youthful gaiety that had lighted up his face even when he was silent was now extinguished.

One day she had finished her darning in the morning and was facing a boring afternoon. Idly she began to wonder if there was not something she could do to relieve her son's misery. Theirs was not a sunny house, but over the roof of the next-door neighbor's godown she could see the tranquil sky of late spring. Making up her mind, she left the house.

She went directly to the breakwater and stood there watching the waves as they dashed themselves to pieces. Like her son, she too went to take counsel with the sea whenever she had something to think about.

The breakwater was covered with the ropes of the octopus pots, spread there to dry. The beach too, now almost empty of boats, was spread with drying nets.

The mother caught sight of a lone butterfly that came flying capriciously from the outspread nets toward the breakwater. It was a large and beautiful black swallowtail. Perhaps the butterfly had come searching for some new and different flower here among the fishing tackle and sand and concrete. The fishermen's houses had no gardens worthy of the name, but only ragged flowerbeds along the narrow, stone-fenced paths, and the butterfly had apparently come to the beach, disgusted with their niggling blossoms.

Beyond the breakwater the waves were always churning up the bottom of the sea, and the water was a muddy yellow-green. And as the waves rolled in, the muddiness was chopped into patterns of tossing bamboo leaves. Presently the mother saw the butterfly take off from the breakwater and fly close to the surface of the muddy water. There it seemed to rest its wings a moment, and then it soared high into the air again.

"What a strange butterfly," she told herself. "It's imitating a sea gull." And at the thought her attention became riveted upon the butterfly.

Soaring high, the butterfly was trying to fly away from the island, directly into the sea-breeze. Mild though it seemed, the breeze tore at the butterfly's tender wings. In spite of it, however, the butterfly, high in the air, finally got clear of the island. The mother stared until it was only a black speck against the dazzling sky.

For a long time the butterfly continued to flutter there in one corner of her field of vision, and then, flying low and hesitantly over the surface of the water, it returned to the breakwater, bewitched by the wideness and glitter of the sea, doubtless driven to despair by the way the next island looked so close and was yet so far.

The butterfly added what appeared to be the shadow of a large knot to the shadow made by one of the drying ropes, and rested its wings.

The mother was not one to put faith in signs and superstitions, and yet the butterfly's futile labor cast a shadow over her heart.

"Foolish butterfly! And if it wants to get away, all it has to do is perch on the ferryboat and go in style."

And yet she herself, having no business in the world outside the island, had not been on the ferryboat now for many, many years.

At this moment for some reason a reckless courage was born within her heart. With firm steps she strode quickly from the breakwater. A diving woman greeted her along the way and was surprised when Shinji's mother walked steadily on as though deep in thought, not even returning the greeting.

Terukichi Miyata was one of the richest men in the village. Of course, about all that could be said of his house was that it was a bit newer than the other village houses. Otherwise it could not even be said that its tile roof towered in particular above the houses around it. The house had neither an outer gate nor a stone wall. Nor was it different from the other houses in its arrangement: the hole for ladling out night soil was to the left of the main door, and the kitchen window to the right, both insisting majestically upon their equal rank, precisely in the same way that the Ministers of the Left and the Right occupy their seats of honor at either side of a Doll Festival arrangement. And yet, being built on a slope, the house did derive a certain air of stability from a stoutly constructed concrete basement on the lower level, where the slope dropped away; this was used as a storeroom and had windows opening directly on the narrow road.

Beside the kitchen door there was a water jar large enough for a man to crawl into. Its wooden lid, under which Hatsue left her letter each morning, gave the outward appearance of protecting the water from dust and dirt, but when summer came it could not keep out the mosquitoes and other flying insects whose dead bodies would suddenly be found floating on the water in the jar.

Shinji's mother hesitated a moment as she was about to enter the house. Just the fact that she had come calling at the Miyata house, where she was not on intimate terms, would be enough to set the villagers' tongues to wagging. She looked about; there was not a human form to be seen. There was nothing but a few chickens scratching in the alley and the color of the sea below, glimpsed through the scanty azalea blossoms of the next house.

The mother put her hand to her hair and, finding it still disarranged from the sea-breeze, took from her bosom a small, red celluloid comb with several teeth missing and quickly combed her hair. She was wearing her everyday work-clothes. Beneath her face, which was bare of any make-up, there was the beginning of her sunburned chest; then came her kimono-like jacket and bloomer-like work-pants, both with many patches, and the wooden clogs on her bare feet.

Her toes had been toughened by the repeated cuts and bruises they had received from the diving women's customary way of always kicking off against the floor of the sea when ready to surface, and the nails were thick and badly twisted; her feet could in no way have been called beautiful, but when planted on the earth they were firm and unshakable.

She opened the door and entered the central work-room. Several pairs of clogs had been taken off and dropped pellmell on the earthen floor, one lying upside down. A pair with red thongs seemed to have just returned from a trip to the sea; wet sand in the shape of footprints was still clinging to the surface of each clog.

The house was filled with silence, and the odor of the toilet floated on the air. The rooms opening off the earthen floor were dark, but sunlight was streaming in through a window somewhere at the back of the house and had spread a bright patch, like a saffron-colored wrapping cloth, in the middle of the floor of one of the farther rooms.

"Good day," the mother called.

She waited awhile. There was no answer. She called again.

Hatsue came down the ladder-like steps at the side of the earth-floored room.

"Why, Auntie!" she said. She was wearing quiet-colored work-pants, and her hair was tied with a yellow ribbon.

"That's a pretty ribbon," the mother complimented her. As she spoke she made a thorough inspection of this girl for whom her son was so lovesick.

It may have been her imagination, but Hatsue's face seemed a little haggard, her complexion a little pale. And because of this her black eyes, clear and shining, seemed all the more prominent.

Becoming aware of the other's scrutiny, Hatsue blushed.

The mother was firm in her courage. She would meet Terukichi, champion her son's innocence, lay bare her heart, and get the two married. The only solution to the situation was for the two parents to talk it over face to face. . . .

"Is your father at home?"

"Yes, he is."

"I've something to talk over with him. Will you please tell him so?"

"Just a minute."

Hatsue climbed the stairs, an uneasy expression on her face.

The mother took a seat on the step leading up from the earthen room into the house proper. . . .

She waited a long time, wishing she had brought cigarettes with her. And as she waited her courage drooped. She began to realize what folly her imagination had led her into.

The stairs creaked softly as Hatsue started down. But she did not come all the way. She called from mid-stairs, seeming to bend her body slightly. The stairs were dark and her face could not be seen clearly as she looked down.

"Uh . . . Father says he won't see you. . . ."

"He won't see me?"

"That's right, but . . ."

With this reply the mother's courage was utterly crushed, and her feeling of humiliation spurred her to a fit of passion. In a flash she recalled her long life of sweat and toil, all the hardships she had faced as a widow. Then, in a tone of voice that sounded as though she were spitting in someone's face—but not until she was already half out the front door—she bawled out:

"All right then! So you say you don't want to see a poor widow. You mean you don't want me to cross your threshold ever again. Well, let me tell you something—and

you tell that father of yours—hear! Tell him I said it first
—that never in my life will I ever cross his damned
threshold again!"

The mother could not bring herself to tell her son
about this fiasco of hers. Looking for a scapegoat, she
turned her spite against Hatsue and said such bad things
about her that, instead of having helped her son, she had
a quarrel with him.

Mother and son did not speak to each other for one
whole day, but then the next day they made up. Thereupon the mother, suddenly overcome with the desire for
her son's sympathy, told him all about her abortive call
on Terukichi. As for Shinji, he had already learned of it
from one of Hatsue's letters.

In her confession the mother omitted the final scene,
in which she had spewed forth those outrageous parting
words of hers, and Hatsue's letter also, out of considera-
tion for Shinji's feelings, had made no mention of this. So
for Shinji there was nothing but the smarting thought of
how his mother had had to eat the humiliation of being
turned away from Terukichi's door. And the soft-hearted
boy told himself that, even if he could not agree with
the bad things his mother said about Hatsue, still he
could not blame her for saying them. Until now he had
never tried to hide his love for Hatsue from his mother,
but he made up his mind that henceforth he must never
confide in anyone except the master and Ryuji. It was out
of devotion for his mother that he made this decision.

Thus it came about that, because she had tried to do
a good deed and had failed, the mother was lonelier than
ever.

.   .   .

It was fortunate that there was not a single day of rest from fishing, for if there had been, it would have served only to make him bemoan the tedium of a day in which he could not meet Hatsue. Thus the month of May came, and their meetings were still prohibited. Then one day Ryuji brought a letter which made Shinji wild with joy:

"*. . . Tomorrow night, for a wonder, Father is having visitors. They're some prefectural officials from Tsu and will spend the night. Whenever Father has guests he always drinks a lot and goes to bed early. So I think it'll be safe for me to slip out of the house about eleven o'clock. Please wait for me in front of Yashiro Shrine. . . .*"

When Shinji returned from fishing that day he changed into a new shirt. His mother, given no explanation, sat looking up at him nervously. She felt as though she were once more looking at her son on that day of the storm.

Shinji had now learned well enough the pain of waiting. So he decided it would be better if he let the girl do the waiting this time. But he could not do it. As soon as his mother and Hiroshi were in bed, he went out. It still lacked two hours of eleven o'clock.

He thought maybe he could kill the time by going to the Young Men's Association. Light was shining from the windows of the hut on the beach and he could hear the voices of the boys who were sleeping there. But then he had the feeling that they were gossiping about him, and he went on by.

Going out onto the nighttime breakwater, the boy turned his face to the sea-breeze. As he did so he recalled the white ship he had seen sailing against a background of sunset clouds on the horizon that day when he had first learned Hatsue's identity from Jukichi, recalled the strange feeling he had had as he watched the ship sail away. That had been the "unknown." So long as he had observed the unknown from a distance, his heart had been peaceful, but once he himself had boarded the unknown and set sail, uneasiness and despair, confusion and anguish had joined forces and borne down upon him.

He believed he knew the reason why his heart, which should have been filled with joy at this moment, was instead crushed and unable to move: the Hatsue whom he would meet tonight would probably insist upon some hasty solution or other to their problem. Elopement? But they were living on an isolated island, and if they were to flee by boat, Shinji had no boat of his own nor, even more important, did he have any money. Double suicide then? Even on this island there had been lovers who took that solution. But the boy's good sense repudiated the thought, and he told himself that those others had been selfish persons who thought only of themselves. Never once had he thought about such a thing as dying; and, above all, there was his family to support.

While he had been pondering these matters, time had moved ahead surprisingly fast. This boy who was so inexpert at thinking was surprised to discover that one of the expected properties of thought was its efficacy as a time-killer. Nevertheless the strong-willed young man abruptly turned off his thoughts: no matter how efficacious it might be, what he had discovered above all else about this new habit of thinking was that it also comprised point-blank peril.

Shinji did not have a watch. As a matter of fact, he needed none. In its place he was endowed with the marvelous ability of being able to sense what time it was instinctively, day or night.

For instance, the stars moved. And even if he was not an expert at measuring their changes precisely, still his body perceived the turning of the immense wheel of the night, the revolution of the giant wheel of the day. Placed as he was, close to the workings of nature, it was not surprising that he should understand nature's precise system.

But, to tell the truth, as he sat on the stairs at the entrance to the office of Yashiro Shrine he had already heard the clock give the single stroke of the half-hour and so was doubly sure it was past ten thirty. The priest and his family were fast asleep. Now the boy pressed his ear to the night-shutters of the house and counted, at full length, the eleven strokes that sounded lonesomely from the wall clock inside.

The boy stood up and, passing through the dark shadows of the pine trees, came to a stop at the top of the flight of two hundred stone steps leading downward to the village. There was no moon, thin clouds covered the sky, and only an occasional star was to be seen. And yet the limestone steps gathered together every last gleam of the night's faint light and, looking like some immense, majestic cataract, fell away from the spot where Shinji stood.

The vast expanse of the Gulf of Ise was completely hidden by the night, but lights could be seen on the farther shores, sparse along the Chita and Atsumi peninsulas, but beautifully and thickly clustered about the city of Uji-Yamada.

The boy was proud of the brand-new shirt he was wearing. He felt sure that its unparalleled whiteness would immediately catch the eye even from the bottommost of the two hundred steps. About halfway down the stone steps there crouched a black shadow, caused by the pine branches that hung over both sides of the stairway there. . . .

A human figure came into view at the bottom of the steps, looking very small. Shinji's heart pounded with joy. The sound of the wooden clogs running determinedly up the steps echoed with a loudness out of all proportion to the smallness of the figure. The footsteps sounded tireless.

Shinji resisted the desire to run down the steps to meet her. After all, since he had waited so long, he had the right to stay calmly at the top. Probably, however, when she came close enough for him to see her face, the only way he could keep from shouting out her name in a loud voice would be to go running down to her. When would he be able to see her face clearly? At about the hundredth step? What—

At that instant Shinji heard a strange roar of anger from below. The voice seemed for certain to be calling Hatsue's name.

Hatsue came to an abrupt halt on the hundredth step, which was slightly wider than the others. He could see her breast moving.

Her father came out of the shadows where he had been hiding. He caught his daughter by the wrist, and Shinji watched them exchange a few violent words. He stood motionless at the top of the steps as though bound there. Terukichi never once so much as glanced in Shinji's direction. Still holding his daughter's wrist, he started down the steps.

Not knowing what he ought to do and feeling as though even his head was half-paralyzed, the boy continued to stand in the same motionless posture, like a sentinel at the top of the stone steps.

The figures of the father and daughter reached the bottom of the steps, turned to the right, and disappeared from view.

## 13

THE YOUNG GIRLS of the island faced the arrival of the diving season with precisely the same heart-strangling feeling city youths have when confronted by final school-term examinations. Their games of scrambling for pebbles on the bottom of the sea close to the beach, begun during the early years of grade school, first introduced them to the art of diving, and they naturally became more skillful as their spirit of rivalry increased. But when they finally began diving for a living and their carefree games turned into real work, without exception the young girls became frightened, and the arrival of spring meant only that the dreaded summer was approaching.

There was the cold, the strangling feeling of running out of breath, the inexpressible agony when water forced its way under the water-goggles, the panic and sudden fear of collapsing that invaded the entire body just when an abalone was almost at the fingertips. There were also all kinds of accidents; and the wounds inflicted on the tips of the toes when kicking off against the sea's bottom, with its carpet of sharp-edged shells, to rise to the surface; and the leaden languor that possessed the body after it had been forced to dive almost beyond endurance. . . . All these things had become sharper and sharper in the remembering; the terror had become all the more intense in the repeating. And often sudden nightmares would awaken the girls from sleep so deep as seemingly to leave no room for dreams to creep in. Then, in the dead of night, in the darkness surrounding their peaceful, danger-less beds, they would peer at the flood of sweat clenched within their fists.

It was different with the older divers, with those who had husbands. Coming out of the water from diving, they would sing and laugh and talk in loud voices. It seemed as though work and play had become united in a single whole for them. Watching them enviously, the young girls would tell themselves that they could never become like that, and yet as the years passed they would be surprised to discover that, without their quite realizing it, they themselves had reached the point where they too could be counted among those lighthearted, veteran divers.

The divers of Uta-jima were at their busiest during June and July. Their operations centered about Garden Beach, on the eastern side of Benten Promontory.

One day, before the onset of the rainy season, the beach lay under a strong, noonday sun that could no longer be called that of early summer. A drying-fire had been lit, and a southerly breeze was carrying its smoke in the direction of the ancient grave-mound of Prince Deki. Garden Beach embraced a small cove, directly beyond which there stretched the Pacific. Summer clouds were towering over the distant sea.

As its name suggested, Niwa-hama—Garden Beach—did indeed have the qualities of a landscaped park. Many limestone crags surrounded the beach, seeming to have been arranged purposely in order that children could hide themselves and fire their pistols in games of cowboys and Indians; moreover, the surfaces of the rocks were smooth to the touch, with occasional finger-size holes as dwellings for crabs and sea-lice. The sand held in the arms of these crags was pure white. Atop the cliff facing the sea to the left the flowers called beach-cotton were in full bloom; their blossoms were not those of the season's end, looking like disheveled sleepers, but were vividly white petals, sensuous and leek-like, brandished against the cobalt sky.

It was the noonday rest period and the area around the fire was noisy with laughing banter. The sand was not yet so hot as to scorch the soles of the feet and, though cold, the water was no longer of that freezing temperature that made the divers rush to put on their padded garments and huddle around the fire the minute they emerged from the sea.

Laughing boisterously, all the divers were thrusting out their chests, boastfully exhibiting their breasts. One of them started to lift her breasts in both hands.

"No, no, it's no fair using your hands. There's no telling how much you might cheat if you used your hands."

"Listen to who's talking! Why, with those breasts of yours you couldn't cheat even if you *did* use your hands."

Everybody laughed. They were arguing as to who had the best-shaped breasts.

All of their breasts were well tanned, and if they lacked the quality of mysterious whiteness, still less did they have the transparent skin that reveals a tracery of veins. Judging merely by the skin, there seemed to be no particular indication of any sensitivity. But beneath the sunburned skin the sun had created a lustrous, semi-transparent color like that of honey. The dark areolas of the nipples did not stand out as isolated spots of black, moist mystery, but instead shaded off gradually into this honey color.

Among the many breasts jostling around the fire there were some which already hung slack and others whose last vestiges remained only in form of dry, hard nipples. But in most cases there were well-developed pectoral muscles, which supported the breasts on firm, wide chests, without letting them droop under their own weight. Their appearance bespoke the fact that these breasts had developed each day beneath the sun, without any knowledge of shame, like ripening fruit.

One of the girls lamented the fact that one of her breasts was smaller than the other, but an outspoken old woman consoled her:

"That's nothing to worry about. Any day now there'll be some handsome young swain to pet them into shape for you."

Everyone laughed again, but the girl still seemed to be worried.

"Are you sure, Grandma Ohara?" she asked.

"I'm sure. I knew a girl like that once before, but once she got herself a man, her breasts evened right up."

Shinji's mother was proud of the fact that her own breasts were still young and fresh, the most youthful among the married women of her age. As though they had never known the hunger of love or the pains of life, all summer long her breasts turned their faces toward the sun, deriving there, first-hand, their inexhaustible strength.

The breasts of the young girls did not particularly arouse her jealousy. There was, however, one beautiful pair that had become the object of everyone's admiration, including that of Shinji's mother. These were the breasts of Hatsue.

This was the first day Shinji's mother had come out to dive. So it was also her first opportunity to have a leisurely look at Hatsue. Even after she had hurled those insulting parting words at Hatsue, they had kept exchanging nods whenever they happened to meet, but Hatsue was by nature not a talkative person. Today again they had been busy with one thing and another and had not had many opportunities for speaking with each other. Even now during the breast-beautiful contest it was mainly the older women who were doing all the talking, and so Shinji's mother, already prejudiced anyway, purposely avoided getting into conversation with Hatsue.

But when she looked at Hatsue's breasts she nodded to herself, understanding why with the passage of time the ugly rumor about the girl and Shinji had died out. No woman who saw those breasts could have any more doubts. Not only were they the breasts of a girl who had never known a man, but they had just begun to bloom, making one think how beautiful they would be once they were in full flower.

Between two small mounds that held on high their rose-colored buds there was a valley that, though darkly burned by the sun, still had not lost the delicacy, the smoothness, the veined coolness of skin—a valley fragrant with thoughts of early spring. Keeping pace with the normal growth of the rest of her body, her breasts were in no way late in their development. Yet their roundness, still tinged with the firmness of childhood, seemed on the verge of awakening from sleep, seemed ready to come awake at the slightest touch of a feather, at the caress of the slightest breeze.

The old grandmother could not resist the impulse to lay her hand against the nipples of these breasts that were so healthily virginal and, at the same time, so exquisitely formed. The touch of her rough palm made Hatsue jump to her feet.

Everyone laughed.

"So now do you understand how men must feel about them, Grandma Ohara?" someone asked.

The old woman rubbed her own wrinkle-covered breasts with both hands and then spoke in a cracking voice:

"What're you talking about? Hers are just green peaches, but mine—mine are well-seasoned pickles. They've soaked up a lot of delicious flavor, let me tell you."

Hatsue laughed and tossed her head. A piece of green, transparent seaweed fell from her hair to the dazzling sand.

While they were all eating their lunches, a favorite man of theirs suddenly appeared from behind some rocks where he had been awaiting what he knew would be the propitious moment.

The women all screamed for the sake of screaming, put their lunches back into the bamboo-leaf wrappers on the ground beside them, and covered their breasts. Actually, they were not in the slightest taken aback. The intruder was an old peddler who made his way to the island every season, and their pretense at bashfulness was nothing but their way of poking fun at his old age.

The old man was wearing a seedy pair of trousers and a white, open-necked shirt. He put down on a rock the big cloth-wrapped bundle he was carrying on his back and wiped the sweat from his face.

"I guess I gave you an awful scare, didn't I? Maybe it was wrong of me to come like this. Shall I go away?"

The peddler said this in full confidence that they would never let him go. He well knew that there was no better way of arousing the divers' desire to buy than by exhibiting his goods here on the beach. The divers always felt bold and open-handed when they were beside the sea. So he would have them choose what they wanted to buy here, and then the same night he would deliver the goods to their homes and collect his money. The women too liked it this way because they could judge colors better in the sunlight.

The old peddler spread his wares out in the shade of some rocks. Still cramming the lunches into their mouths, the women crowded around the display.

There were lengths of stencil-dyed cotton material for summer kimonos. There were light housedresses and children's clothes. There were unlined sashes, underpants, undershirts, and sash strings.

The peddler took the lid off a flat wooden box, and cries of admiration escaped from the women's mouths. The

box was filled to overflowing with beautiful notions—
coin purses, clog thongs, plastic handbags, ribbons,
brooches, and the like, all in assorted colors.

"There's not a thing there I wouldn't like to have," one
of the young divers truthfully remarked.

In a flash many sun-blackened fingers reached out; the
goods were painstakingly examined and criticized; argu-
ments broke out among the women as to whether something was or was not becoming to so-and-so; and half-
joking bargaining grew apace. As a result the peddler sold
two lengths of summer-kimono material in tawdry, towel-
like patterns at almost a thousand yen each, as well as one
unlined sash of a mixed weave, and a large amount of
sundry merchandise. Shinji's mother bought a plastic shop-
ping-bag for two hundred yen, and Hatsue bought a
length of the better cotton-kimono material, in a youthful pattern of dark-blue morning-glories on a white background.

The old peddler was pleased with all this unexpectedly
good business. He was quite gaunt, and his sunburned ribs
could be seen through the open collar of his shirt.
His pepper-and-salt hair was cut short, and the years had
deposited a number of dark splotches on his cheeks and
temples. He had only a few straggling tobacco-stained
teeth, which made it difficult to understand what he
said, and still more so now when he raised his voice loudly.
Nevertheless, by the laughter that made his cheeks
tremble as though with a twitch and by his exaggerated
gestures, the women realized that the peddler was about
to render them some magnificent service, "quite apart
from any desire for gain."

With scurrying fingers—he had let the nail grow long

on the little finger of each hand—the peddler produced three beautiful plastic handbags from the box of notions.

"Look! This blue one is for young ladies, this brown for the middle-aged, and this black for ladies of advanced years—"

"I'll take the young ladies' one," the same old woman broke in, and everyone laughed, causing the peddler to raise his quavering voice still higher.

"Plastic handbags of the very latest fashion. Fixed price, eight hundred yen—"

"Oh, they're *dear*, aren't they?"

"Of course; he's padded the price."

"No, no, eight hundred yen without any padding at all. And I'm going to present one of these beautiful handbags to one of you ladies as a token of my appreciation for your kind patronage...absolutely free!"

Dozens of guileless, open hands were simultaneously stretched forth. But the old man brushed them aside with a flourish.

"One, I said. Just one. It's the Omiya Prize, a sort of sacrificial service rendered by my shop, the Omiya Shop, in celebration of the prosperity of Uta-jima Village. We'll have a contest, and one of these bags shall go to whoever wins. The blue if the victor is young, the brown if it's a middle-aged lady . . ."

The diving women were holding their breath. Each was thinking that, with just a little luck, she would receive an eight-hundred-yen handbag for nothing.

The peddler had once been a grade-school principal and often brooded over having come to his present humble circumstances because of a mess he had gotten into with a woman, but now the divers' silence gave him new confidence in his ability to win people's hearts, and once again he told himself that he would quit peddling and become an athletic director.

"Well, then, if we're to have a contest, it ought to be something for the good of Uta-jima Village, to which I owe so much. How about it, everyone—what would you say to an abalone contest? And to the person who brings up the biggest catch in the next hour I'll present the prize."

Ceremoniously he spread a cloth in the shade of another rock and gravely decked it with the prizes. To tell the truth, not one of the handbags was worth more than about five hundred yen, but they looked worth fully eight hundred. The youthful prize was sky-blue and box-shaped, and its cobalt color, bright as a new-built boat, made an inexpressibly lovely contrast with its glittering, gold-plated clasp. The brown, middle-aged one was also box-shaped, and its ostrich-skin pattern had been so exceedingly well pressed into the plastic that at first glance one could not tell whether it was genuine ostrich skin or not. Only the black one, for old ladies, was not box-shaped, but with its long and slender golden clasp and its oblong boat shape, it was indeed a tasteful, refined piece of workmanship.

Shinji's mother, who wanted the brown, middle-aged bag, was the first to announce her name for the contest.

The second person who called out her name was Hatsue.

Carrying the eight divers who had entered the contest, the boat pulled away from the shore. A fat, middle-aged woman, who had not entered the contest, stood in the stern and sculled. Of the eight, Hatsue was the only young girl. All the other girls had held back, knowing they could not win anyway; they were cheering for Hatsue. As for the other women left on the beach, each was shouting encouragement to her own favorite.

The boat took a southward course along the beach and moved away to the eastern side of the island.

The divers who were left behind gathered around the old peddler and sang songs.

The water in the cove was clear and blue, and when the waves were still one could plainly see the round rocks on the bottom, covered with red seaweed and looking as though they were floating close to the surface. Actually, however, they were deeply submerged. The waves swelled large at this point, throwing shadows of their patterns and refractions of froth over the rocks on the ocean floor as they passed over them. Then, no sooner had a wave risen full than it smashed itself to pieces on the beach. Thereupon a reverberation like that of a deep sigh would overflow the entire beach and drown out the women's singing.

An hour later the boat returned from the eastern side of the island. Many times more exhausted than usual because of the competition, the eight divers sat silent in the boat, leaning against one another, each staring out toward whatever direction her eyes happened to fancy. Their wet, disheveled hair was so tangled together that it was impossible to tell one diver's hair from that of her neighbors. Two of them were hugging each other to keep warm. All their breasts were covered with goose flesh, and in the too-brilliant sunshine even their naked, sunburned bodies seemed to turn pale, making them look like a group of pallid, drowned corpses.

The noisy reception they received from the beach was out of keeping with the quietness of this boat that moved so soundlessly forward. The moment they were on land the eight women collapsed on the sand around the fire and would not even speak.

The peddler checked the contents of the buckets he had collected from the divers. When he was done, he called out the results in a loud voice:

"Hatsue-san is first—twenty abalone! And the mistress of the Kubo family is second—eighteen!"

The winner and the runner-up, Hatsue and Shinji's mother, exchanged glances out of tired, bloodshot eyes. The island's most expert diver had been bested by a girl who had learned her skill from the divers of another island.

Hatsue got to her feet in silence and went around the rock to receive her prize. And the prize she returned with was the brown, middle-aged handbag, which she pressed into the hands of Shinji's mother.

The mother's cheeks flushed red with delight.

"But . . . why? . . ."

"Because I've always wanted to apologize ever since my father spoke so rudely to Auntie that day."

"She's a fine girl!" the peddler shouted, and when everyone joined in with unanimous praise of Hatsue, urging the older woman to accept the girl's kindness, Shinji's mother took the brown handbag, wrapped it carefully in a piece of paper, clasped it under a bare arm, and spoke quite casually:

"Why, thanks."

The mother's simple, straightforward heart had immediately understood the modesty and respect behind the girl's gesture. Hatsue smiled, and Shinji's mother told herself how wise her son had been in his choice of a bride. . . . And it was in this same fashion that the politics of the island were always conducted.

146

# 14

For Shinji the rainy reason brought only one bitter
day after another. Even Hatsue's letters had ceased.
Doubtless, after her father had frustrated their meeting at
Yashiro Shrine, which he had probably learned about
by reading her letter, he had absolutely forbidden Hatsue
to write again.

One day before the end of the rains the captain of the
*Utajima-maru* came to the island. The *Utajima-maru* was
the larger of Terukichi Miyata's two coasting freighters
and was now anchored at Toba.

The captain went first to Terukichi's house, and next to
Yasuo's. The same night he went to see Shinji's boss, Jukichi, and then at last went to Shinji's house.

The captain was a few years past forty and had three children. He was a man of big stature and proud of his strength, but he had a gentle disposition. He was a zealous member of the Nichiren sect, and if he happened to be on the island at the time of the Lantern Festival, he would always officiate as a sort of lay priest in reading the *sutras* for the repose of the souls of the dead. He had women in various ports, whom his crew referred to as the Yokohama aunt, the Moji aunt, and the like. Whenever the ship called at one of these ports, the captain would take the young crew members along to his woman's place for a drink. The "aunts" all dressed conservatively and always treated the young men with great kindness.

The gossip was that the captain's half-bald head was the result of his debaucheries. This was the reason he always maintained his dignity with a gold-braided uniform cap.

As soon as the captain reached the house he began discussing his business with Shinji's mother. Shinji too was present.

When the boys of the village reached the age of seventeen or eighteen they began their maritime training in the capacity of "rice-rinsers," the local word for apprentice seamen. And Shinji was at the age to be thinking about it. The captain asked if he would like to join the *Utajima-maru* as a "rice-rinser."

The mother was silent, and Shinji replied that he would give his answer after he had had a chance to discuss it with Jukichi, his boss. The captain said that if it was a question of Jukichi's approval, he had already secured that.

But still there was something strange about it all. The *Utajima-maru* belonged to Terukichi, and there certainly was no reason for him to employ Shinji, whom he disliked so much, as a crew member on one of his own ships.

"No, Uncle Teru himself sees that you'll make a good sailor. As soon as I mentioned you, Uncle Teru agreed. So come on then, do your best and work hard."

To make sure it was all right, Shinji accompanied the captain to Jukichi's house, and Jukichi also strongly urged Shinji to take the job. He said it would be a bit difficult on the *Taihei-maru* without Shinji, but that he couldn't stand in the way of the boy's future. So Shinji agreed.

The next day Shinji heard the startling news that Yasuo too was going to serve an apprenticeship on the *Utajima-maru*. The story went that Yasuo had not at all relished the idea of becoming a "rice-rinser" and had been forced to agree only when Uncle Teru declared that the apprenticeship had to come before any betrothal to Hatsue.

When Shinji heard this, his heart was filled with anxiety, pain, and then, at the same time, hope.

Together with his mother, Shinji went to Yashiro Shrine to pray for a safe voyage and to obtain a charm.

The day of departure had come. Accompanied by the captain, Shinji and Yasuo boarded the *Kamikaze-maru* for the ferry-crossing to Toba. A number of people came to see Yasuo off, including Hatsue, but there was no sign of Terukichi. Shinji was seen off by no one but his mother and Hiroshi.

Hatsue did not look in Shinji's direction. But just as the boat was about to sail, she whispered something to Shinji's mother and handed her a small package. The mother gave it to her son.

Even after he was on the boat Shinji had no chance to

open the package, as the captain and Yasuo were with him. He gazed at the receding outline of Uta-jima. And as he did so he became aware of his own feelings for the first time.

Here he was, a young man born and bred on that island, loving it more than anything else in the world, and yet he was now eager to leave it. It was his desire to leave the island that had made him accept the captain's offer of a berth on the *Utajima-maru.*

Once the island was out of sight the boy's heart became peaceful. As he had never been on his daily fishing trips, he was now free of the thought that tonight he would have to return to the island again.

"I'm free!" he shouted in his heart. This was the first time he had ever realized there could be such a strange sort of freedom as this.

The *Kamikaze-maru* sailed on through a drizzling rain. Yasuo and the captain stretched out on the straw mats in the passenger cabin and went to sleep. Yasuo had not spoken to Shinji once since they had boarded the ferry.

The boy pressed his face close to one of the round portholes, across which the raindrops were running, and by its light examined the contents of the package from Hatsue. It contained another charm from Yashiro Shrine, a snapshot of Hatsue, and a letter. The letter read:

*"Every day from now on I'll be going to Yashiro Shrine to pray for your safety. My heart belongs to you. Please take care of yourself and come back safe and sound. I'm enclosing my picture so I can go voyaging with you. It was taken at Cape Daio. About our voyage—Father hasn't said a word to me, but I think he must have some special reason for putting both you and Yasuo on his ship. And*

*somehow I think I can see a ray of hope for us. Please, please don't give up hope; please keep on fighting."*

The letter encouraged the boy. Strength filled his arms and the feeling that life was worth living flooded through his entire body.

Yasuo was still asleep. By the light from the porthole Shinji studied Hatsue's photograph. In it the girl was leaning against one of Cape Daio's huge pines and a sea-breeze was blowing her skirts, whirling about inside her thin, white summer dress, caressing her bare skin. And his courage was still further revived by the thought that he too had once done just what the wind in the photograph was doing.

Reluctant to take his eyes off the picture, Shinji had propped it up on the edge of the rain-blurred porthole and had stared at it for a long time, when behind it there slowly moved into view the outline of Toshi Island to port. . . .

Once again the boy's heart lost its peacefulness. But the strange way in which love can torture the heart with desire was no longer a novel thing for him.

It had stopped raining by the time they reached Toba. Dull silver rays of light shone down from between rifts in the clouds.

Among the many small fishing-boats in Toba's harbor the one-hundred-and-eighty-five-ton *Utajima-maru* stood out conspicuously. The three jumped down onto its deck, which was sparkling in the sunshine after the rain. Rain-drops were still running gleaming down the white-painted masts, and the imposing booms were folded down over the hatches.

The crew had not yet returned from shore leave. The captain led the two boys to their quarters, an eight-mat cabin next to the master's quarters and directly over the kitchen and mess hall. Other than the lockers and a small central space covered with thin straw matting, there was nothing except two sets of two-tiered bunks on the right and, on the left, one set of bunks and a separate bunk for the chief engineer. Several photographs of movie actresses were stuck to the ceiling like charms.

Shinji and Yasuo were assigned to the first tier of bunks on the right. The chief engineer, the first and second mates, the bosun, the seamen, and the firemen all slept in this one small cabin, but as they alternated the watches, there were always bunks enough to go round at any one time.

After showing them the bridge, the master's quarters, the holds, and the mess hall, the captain left them to rest in the crew's cabin.

Left alone in the cabin, the two looked at each other. Yasuo felt downhearted and decided to make peace.

"Well, here we are at last, just the two of us to be friends. A lot of things happened on the island, but let's forget about them and be good friends from now on."

Shinji gave a grunt of agreement and smiled.

Toward evening the crew returned to the ship. Most of them were from Uta-jima and were known by sight to Shinji and Yasuo. Still smelling of liquor, they all teased the newcomers. Then the two of them were instructed in the daily routine and assigned their various duties.

The ship was to sail at nine in the morning. Shinji was given the task of taking the anchor-light off the mast at the first crack of dawn the next morning. The anchor-light was very much like the night-shutters of a house ashore: turning it off meant that the ship was awake, just as opening the night-shutters means a house is awake.

Shinji scarcely closed his eyes all night and was up before the sun the next morning, taking down the anchor-light as things began to turn gray. The morning was wrapped in a misty rain, and the street lamps of Toba ran in two straight lines from the harbor to the railway station. The thick-throated whistle of a freight train sounded from the direction of the station.

The boy scrambled up the naked mast over the furled sails, used for auxiliary power. The wood was wet and cold, and the rocking motion of the faint waves that lapped the ship's sides was transmitted directly to the mast. In the first rays of the morning sun, wet with mist, the anchor-light was a hazy, milk-white color. The boy reached up for the hook. As though it disliked being taken down, the anchor-light gave a big swing, the flame flickered inside the drenched glass, and a few drops of water fell into the boy's upturned face.

Shinji wondered what port they would be in when he next took down this light.

The *Utajima-maru,* on charter to the Yamagawa Transport Company, was to carry lumber to Okinawa and return to Kobe in about six weeks. After sailing through the Kii Channel and calling at Kobe, the ship sailed westward through the Inland Sea and had its quarantine inspection at Moji. It then proceeded southward along the eastern coast of Kyushu and received its sailing clearance at the port of Nichinan in Miyazaki Prefecture, where there was a Customs office.

The ship then called at the harbor of Fukushima, at the

southern tip of Kyushu. There it took on a cargo of four-teen thousand cubic feet of lumber.

After leaving Fukushima the *Utajima-maru* became in fact a sea-going vessel and was handled as such. It was due to reach Okinawa in about two or two and a half days. . . .

When there was no work to be done with the cargo, or during their rest periods, the crew would loll about on the thin straw matting that covered the three-mat space in the center of their quarters and listen to a portable phonograph. There were only a few records, and most of them were so worn out that they produced only dingy music through the scratching of a rusty needle. Without exception they were all sentimental ballads concerning ports or sailors, fog or memories of women, the Southern Cross or liquor or sighs. The chief engineer was tone-deaf and never succeeded in his efforts to learn at least one tune during a voyage, always forgetting what little he had memorized before the next voyage. Whenever the ship would pitch or roll suddenly, the needle would go sliding across the record, leaving another scratch in its wake.

Often at night they would sit up late arguing ridiculous points. Such subjects as love and marriage, or whether the human body can take as large an injection of salt as of dextrose, were sufficient to keep them talking for hours. The person who maintained his point with the most stubbornness usually won in the end, but the reasoning of Ya-suo, who had been president of the Young Men's Association on the island, was so logical that it even won the respect of his elders. As for Shinji, he always sat silent, hugging his knees and smiling as he listened to the others' opinions.

"There's no doubt but what the boy's a fool," the chief engineer once told the captain.

154

It was a busy life aboard the ship. From the moment the newcomers got up there were always decks for them to clean or some other of their numerous odd jobs to be performed.

It gradually became abundantly clear to the crew that Yasuo was lazy. His attitude was that it was enough just to go through the motions of performing his duties. Shinji, however, covered up for him and even did part of Yasuo's work, so this attitude of his did not become immediately apparent to his superiors.

But one morning the bosun, finding Yasuo loafing in the cabin after having stolen away from his deck-cleaning duties on the pretext of going to the head, lost his temper and berated him roundly.

Yasuo gave a most ill-considered reply:

"Oh well, anyway, when this voyage is over I'm going to become Uncle Teru's son. Then this ship will belong to me."

The bosun was in a rage, but he prudently held his tongue, telling himself it just might turn out the way Yasuo said. He never again scolded Yasuo to his face, but from his whispered words the other men soon learned what the insubordinate youngster had said, and the result was all to Yasuo's disadvantage rather than otherwise.

Shinji was extremely busy, and the only chance he had to look at Hatsue's picture was a brief moment each night before going to bed or when he was on watch. He never let anyone else so much as set eyes on the picture. One day when Yasuo was bragging about being adopted by Terukichi as Hatsue's husband, Shinji took what was for him a most unusually devious means of revenge. He asked Yasuo if he had a photograph of Hatsue.

"Sure I have," Yasuo replied immediately.

Shinji knew without a doubt that this was a lie and his heart was filled with glee.

A few moments later Yasuo spoke very nonchalantly. "Do you have one too?" he asked.

"Have one what?"

"A picture of Hatsue."

"No, I don't have one."

This was probably the first deliberate lie Shinji had ever told in his life.

The *Utajima-maru* arrived at Naha. After clearing quarantine, it entered the harbor and discharged its cargo. It was forced to lie at anchor two or three days, waiting and waiting for permission to enter the closed port of Unten, where it was to load scrap metal for the return voyage to Japan. Unten was on the northern tip of Okinawa, where the American forces had made their first landing in the war.

Since the crew were not allowed ashore, they spent their time staring from the deck out at the desolate, barren hills. The Americans had burned down every tree on the hills when they landed, fearing unexploded mines.

The Korean war had come to an end for the time being, but in the crew's eyes the island still had a most unusual air. From morning to night there was the droning thunder of fighter planes practicing, and countless vehicles, gleaming in the sun of a tropical summer, were constantly moving back and forth along the broad, paved highway that bordered the harbor—sedans and trucks and various military vehicles. Beside the road, the prefabricated houses for families of American military personnel were aglint with the color of new cement, while the patched tin roofs of the battered native houses were ugly blotches on the landscape.

The only person who went ashore—to get the agent for Yamagawa Transport to send a chandler—was the first mate.

At last the permit to enter Unten was received. The *Utajima-maru* entered the port and took on its cargo of scrap. They had just finished when the report came that Okinawa was in the path of a threatening typhoon. Hoping to escape the typhoon by sailing as quickly as possible, they cleared port early the next morning. Then all the ship had to do was lay its course straight for Japan.

That morning a light rain was falling. The waves were high and the winds southwesterly. The hills quickly vanished from view behind them, and the *Utajima-maru* sailed on by compass for six hours, with very poor visibility. The barometer fell steadily and the waves became still higher. The atmospheric pressure reached an abnormal low.

The captain decided to return to Unten. The rain was blown to mist by the wind, visibility had gone down to absolute zero, and the six-hour run back to port was extremely difficult.

Finally the hills of Unten were sighted. The bosun, who was quite familiar with these waters, stood on lookout in the bow. The harbor was enclosed by about two miles of coral reef, and the channel through the reef, not even marked with buoys, was most difficult to navigate.

"Stop! . . . Go! . . . Stop! . . . Go! . . ."

Checking its headway countless times and then moving ahead very slowly, the ship passed through the channel between the coral reefs. It was then six o'clock in the evening.

One bonito ship had taken shelter within the reefs. Fastening themselves together with several ropes, the two ships proceeded side by side into Unten's harbor.

The waves in the harbor were low, but the wind grew always stronger. Still side by side, the *Utajima-maru* and the bonito ship threw out four lines each—two hawsers and two cables—tying their bows to a buoy the size of a small room, and prepared to ride out the storm.

The *Utajima-maru* had no radio equipment, depending solely upon its compass. So the radio operator on the bonito ship passed on to them every report he received concerning the typhoon's development and course.

When night came the bonito ship put out a deck watch of four men and the *Utajima-maru* put out a three-man watch. Their duty was to watch the hawsers and cables, as one could never be sure they might not snap at any moment.

There was also the uneasy feeling that the buoy itself might not hold. But the danger of snapping lines was much the greater. Fighting the wind and the waves, the watch courted death many times to keep the ropes wet with salt water, fearing they might fray if they became too dry in the wind.

By nine o'clock that night the two ships were beset by a wind with a speed of fifty-six miles an hour.

An hour before midnight Shinji and Yasuo and one of the young seamen took the watch. Their bodies were hurled against the wall as soon as they began crawling out onto the deck. The wind-whipped rain struck their cheeks as though it were needles.

It was impossible to stand upright on the deck, which rose up like a wall before their very eyes. Every timber of the ship was creaking and rumbling. The waves in the harbor were not quite high enough to sweep the decks, but the spray of the waves, blown on the wind, had become a billowing mist, shrouding their vision. Crawling along the deck, the three finally reached the prow and clung to the bitts there. The two hawsers and two cables that secured the ship to the buoy were tied to these bitts.

They could see the buoy dimly about twenty-five yards away in the night, just barely revealing its white-painted existence through the pervading darkness. And when, to the accompaniment of the creaking of the cables, which was like shrieks, a huge mass of wind would strike the ship and lift it high into the air, the buoy would fall far below them into the blackness and seem all the smaller.

The three looked at each other's faces as they clung to the bitts, but they did not speak. And the salt water striking their faces made it all but impossible for them even to keep their eyes open. The neighing of the wind and the roar of the sea, surprisingly enough, gave the infinite night that enveloped them a quality of frenzied serenity.

Their job was to keep their eyes riveted on the lines tying the *Utajima-maru* to the buoy. Stretched taut, the hawsers and cables drew the only indomitably straight lines across a scene in which everything else was pitching and rolling with the gale's madness. The way they stared fixedly at these rigidly drawn lines created in their hearts a feeling akin to confidence, born of their very concentration.

There were times when it seemed as if the wind had

suddenly stopped, but instead of reassuring them, such moments made the three young men shiver with terror. Instantly the huge mass of the wind would come crashing again, rattling the yardarms and thrusting the atmosphere aside with a tremendous roar.

The three continued their silent watch over the lines. Even above the sound of the wind they could hear intermittently the shrill and piercing creaking of the lines.

"Look!" Yasuo cried in a thin voice.

One of the cables wrapped around the bitts was rasping ominously; it seemed to be slipping a little. The bitts were directly before their eyes, and they perceived an extremely slight but sinister alteration in the way the lines were wrapped about the bitts.

At that instant a length of cable came recoiling out of the darkness, flashing like a whip, and hit the bitts with a snarling sound.

They had dodged instantly, just in time to escape being slashed by the severed cable, which had force enough to have cut them to the bone. Like some living thing that takes long in dying, the cable writhed about in the darkness of the deck, making a shrill noise. Finally it came to rest in a semicircle.

When they finally grasped the situation, the three young men turned pale. One of the four lines tying the ship to the buoy had given way. And no none could guarantee that the cable and two hawsers that remained might not give way also at any moment.

"Let's tell the captain," Yasuo said, moving away from the bitts.

Searching for handholds as he went creeping along, being thrown off his feet many times, Yasuo groped his way to the bridge and made his report to the captain.

The burly captain remained calm, or at least gave the outward appearance of doing so.

"I see. Well, then, let's just use a lifeline. The typhoon passed its peak at one o'clock, so there's no danger at all in using a lifeline now. Someone can just swim out to the buoy and tie the lifeline to it."

Leaving the second mate in charge of the bridge, the captain and the chief mate followed Yasuo back. Like mice tugging at a rice cake, they rolled and dragged a lifeline and a new marline along with them step by step from the bridge to the bow bitts.

Shinji and the sailor looked up at them inquiringly. The captain stooped over them and shouted to the three youths in a loud voice:

"Which one of you fellows is going to take this lifeline over there and tie it to that buoy?"

The roaring of the wind covered the youths' silence.

"Don't any of you have any guts?" the captain shouted again.

Yasuo's lips quivered. He pulled his neck down into his shoulders.

Then Shinji shouted out in a cheerful voice, and as he did so the white flash of his teeth shone through the blackness to prove that he was smiling.

"I'll do it," he shouted clearly.

"Good! Go ahead!"

Shinji rose to his feet. He was ashamed of himself for the way he had been squatting on the deck until now, practically cowering. The wind came attacking out of the black reaches of the night, striking him full in the body, but to Shinji, accustomed to rough weather in a small fishing-boat, the heaving deck on which his feet were firmly planted was nothing but a stretch of earth that was frankly a bit out of sorts.

He stood listening.

The typhoon was directly above the boy's gallant head. It was as right for Shinji to be invited to a seat at this banquet of madness as to a quiet and natural afternoon nap.

Inside his raincoat the sweat was running so profusely that both his back and chest were drenched. He took the raincoat off and threw it aside. As he did so his barefoot figure, wearing a white T shirt, loomed through the blackness of the storm.

Under the captain's directions, the men tied one end of the lifeline to the bitts and the other end to the marline. Hindered by the wind, the operation progressed slowly.

When the ropes were finally tied, the captain handed the free end of the marline to Shinji and yelled into his ear:

"Tie this around your waist and swim for it! When you reach the buoy, haul the lifeline over and make it fast!"

Shinji wrapped the marline twice around his waist above his belt. Then, standing in the bow, he stared down at the sea. Down beneath the spray, down beneath the whitecaps that beat themselves to pieces against the prow, there were the jet-black, invisible waves, twisting and coiling their bodies. They kept repeating their patternless movements, concealing their incoherent and perilous whims. No sooner would one seem about to come rising into sight than it would drop away to become a whirling, bottomless abyss again.

At this point there flashed across Shinji's mind the

thought of Hatsue's photograph in the inside pocket of his coat hanging in the crew's quarters. But this idle thought was blown to bits upon the wind.

He dived from the prow of the ship.

The buoy was about twenty-five yards away. Despite his great physical strength, which he was confident would have to yield to none, and despite too his ability to swim around his home island five times without stopping, still it seemed impossible that these would suffice to get him across the immensity of those twenty-five yards.

A terrible force was upon the boy's arms; something like an invisible bludgeon belabored them as they tried to cut a way through the waves. In spite of himself, his body was tossed on the waves, and when he tried to bring his strength into opposition to the waves and grapple with them, his movements were as useless as though he were trying to run through grease.

He would be certain that the buoy was finally within arm's reach, and when he rose up out of the trough of the next wave he would look for it—and find it just as far away as ever.

The boy swam with all his might. And, inch by inch, step by step, the huge mass of the enemy fell back, opening the way for him. It was as though a drill were boring its way through the hardest of solid rock.

The first time his hand touched the buoy he lost his hold and was pulled away. But then by good luck a wave swept him forward again and, just as it seemed on the point of dashing his chest against the iron rim, lifted him up with a single sweep and deposited him on the buoy.

Shinji took a deep breath, and the wind filled his nostrils and mouth to the choking point. At that instant it seemed to him that he could never breathe again, and for a time he even forgot the task he was supposed to perform.

The buoy rolled and pitched, surrendering its body openheartedly to the black sea. The waves ceaselessly washed over half of it, pouring off with great commotion.

Lying face down so as not to be blown off by the wind, Shinji started untying the line from around his waist. The knot was wet and difficult to loosen. When it was finally untied, he began pulling the marline.

Now for the first time he looked toward the ship. He could see the forms of the four men clustered about the bow bitts. The men on watch in the bow of the bonito ship also were gazing steadily in his direction. Although only a scant twenty-five yards away, everything seemed exceedingly distant. The black shadows of the two moored ships were rising together, side by side, high into the air, and then sinking back into the waves again.

The thin marline offered little resistance to the wind and was comparatively easy to haul in, but soon a heavy weight was added to its end. It was the lifeline, almost five inches thick, which he was now pulling. Shinji was all but thrown forward into the sea.

The wind resistance against the lifeline was very strong, but at last the boy had one end of it in his hands. It was so thick that even one of his big hands would not go entirely around it.

Shinji was at a loss as to how to apply his strength. He wanted to brace himself with his feet to pull, but the wind would not permit that posture. And when he heedlessly applied all his strength to the rope, he was all but dragged into the sea. His drenched body was at fever heat, his face burning hot, and his temples were throbbing violently.

He finally managed to wind the lifeline once around the buoy; then the operation became easier. The line provided him with a fulcrum for his strength, and now for a change he could support his body with the thick line.

He wound the line once more around the buoy and then proceeded methodically to tie it fast. He waved his arms to announce the successful completion of the job.

He could plainly see the four men on the ship waving their arms in reply. The boy forgot how exhausted he was. His instinct for cheerfulness reasserted itself and flagging energy welled up anew. Facing into the storm, he inhaled his fill of air and then dived into the sea for the return trip.

They lowered a net from the deck and hoisted Shinji aboard. Once the boy was back on deck, the captain clapped him on the shoulder with a huge hand. Although Shinji was ready to faint with fatigue, his masculine energy still maintained him.

The captain had Yasuo help Shinji to his quarters and the men who were off duty wiped him dry. The boy fell asleep the moment he was in his bunk. No noise the storm could make could have disturbed that deep sleep. . . .

The next morning Shinji opened his eyes to find brilliant sunshine falling across his pillow. Through the round port-hole in his bunk he looked out at the crystal-clear blue sky that followed the typhoon's departure, at the view of bald hills under a tropical sun, at the glitter of a placid, undisturbed sea.

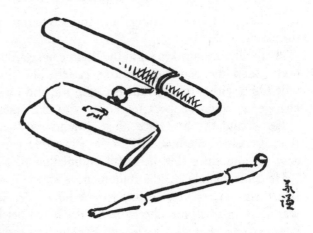

## 15

THE *Utajima-maru* returned to Kobe several days behind schedule. So by the time the captain and Shinji and
Yasuo reached the island, where they were to have returned before mid-August, in time for the lunar-calendar
Lantern Festival, the festivities were already over.

They heard the news of the island while being ferried
across on the *Kamikaze-maru*. A huge turtle had come
ashore on Five League Beach a few days before the
Lantern Festival and had been quickly killed. There were
more than a basketful of eggs in it, which had been sold
for two yen apiece.

Shinji went to worship at Yashiro Shrine, to give thanks
for his safe return, and then on to Jukichi's, where he
had been immediately invited for a celebration. Over

the protests of the boy, who never drank, his saké cup was filled many times.

Two days later he once again went out fishing on Jukichi's boat. Shinji had not said anything about his voyage, but Jukichi had heard all the details from the captain.

"I hear you did a great thing."

"Oh, no." The boy blushed a little, but had nothing further to say. Anyone unfamiliar with his personality might easily have concluded that he had spent the last month and a half off sleeping somewhere.

Jukichi was silent awhile and then spoke in an offhand way:

"Have you heard anything from Uncle Teru?"

"No."

"Oh."

No one made any mention of Hatsue, and Shinji, feeling no great loneliness, threw himself into the old familiar work, while the boat rocked in the rough seas of the dog days. The work fit both his body and soul perfectly, like a well-tailored suit, leaving no room for the intrusion of other worries.

The strange feeling of self-sufficiency did not leave him all day. At dusk he saw the outline of a white freighter sailing far out at sea, and it was different from that he had seen on that day so long ago, but once again Shinji felt a new emotion.

"I know where that ship is bound for," he thought. "I know what sort of life they live aboard it, what sort of hardships they have. I know everything about that ship."

At least, the white ship was no longer a shadow of the unknown. Instead, there was that about the distant white freighter, trailing its long plume of smoke through the late-summer dusk, that quickened his heart even more than had the unknown. The boy felt again in his hands the weight of that lifeline he had pulled with the last ounce of his strength. With these strong hands he had certainly once actually touched that "unknown" at which he had previously stared from a great distance. He had the sensation that now, by simply stretching out his hand, he could touch that white ship out at sea.

On a childish impulse, he held his five big-knuckled fingers out toward the sea to the east, already thick with the shadows of evening clouds. . . .

Summer vacation was half over, and still Chiyoko did not come home. The lighthouse-keeper and his wife waited day by day for their daughter's return to the island. The mother wrote an urgent letter. No reply came. She wrote again. Ten days later there was a grudging answer. Giving no reason, Chiyoko simply wrote that she would not be able to come back to the island during this vacation.

The mother finally decided to try tears as a means of persuasion and sent a special-delivery letter of more than ten pages, pouring out her feelings and begging her daughter to come home. A reply came when only a few days remained of vacation and a week after Shinji's return to the island. It was a reply which the startled mother had never dreamed of.

In her letter Chiyoko confessed how she had seen Shinji and Hatsue coming down the stone stairs arm in arm that day of the storm, and how she had then landed the two of them in great difficulties by the uncalled-for act of running to Yasuo with the tale. Chiyoko was still tormented with feelings of guilt, and she went on to say that unless Shinji and Hatsue finally found their happiness, she herself would be too ashamed ever to come back to the island. If her mother would act as a go-between and persuade Terukichi to let them get married . . . This was the condition she set for her return to the island.

This tragic, demandingly badgering letter sent chills up the kind-hearted mother's spine. She was struck with the thought that, unless she took appropriate steps, her daughter, unable to bear the pangs of conscience, might even commit suicide. From her wide reading the mistress of the lighthouse recalled various frightening instances of adolescent girls who had killed themselves over some equally trivial matter.

She decided not to show the letter to her husband, the lighthouse-keeper, and told herself that every day counted, that by herself she would have to manage everything at once in such a way as to bring her daughter home as quickly as possible.

As she changed into her best clothes, a suit of white cambric, there was reborn within her the mettlesome feeling of years gone by when, as a teacher in a girls' high school, she was on her way to complain to some parent about a problem student.

Straw mats were spread out in front of the houses along the roadside leading down into the village, and on them there were sesame and red beans and soy beans drying in the sun. The tiny green sesame seed, washed by the late-summer sun, cast their miniature, spindle-shaped shadows one by one across the coarse straw of the fresh-colored mats.

From here one could look down upon the sea. The waves were not running high today.

As the mother descended the steps that formed the main street of the village, her white shoes made light sounds against the concrete. Then she began to hear lively, laughing voices and the springy sound of wet clothes being beaten.

She drew nearer the sounds and found a half-dozen women in housedresses doing their laundry by the side of the stream bordering the road. Shinji's mother was one of the group.

After the Lantern Festival the diving women had more leisure, going out only occasionally to gather edible seaweed, so they turned then to an energetic washing of the accumulation of dirty clothes. Using almost no soap, they one and all would spread the laundry over flat rocks and trample it with their feet.

"Why, hello, mistress. Where are you on your way to today?"

They all bowed and called out their greetings. Beneath their tucked-up skirts the water reflections were playing over their dark thighs.

"I just thought I'd drop by Terukichi Miyata-san's place a minute."

As she made this reply, it occurred to her that it would be strange to meet Shinji's mother this way and then, without so much as a word to her, proceed on to arrange for her son's engagement. So she turned and started down the precipitous flight of slippery, moss-covered stone steps that led from the road to the stream. Her shoes made the descent perilous, so, turning her back to the water, but stealing many a glance over her shoulder, she backed slowly down the steps on all fours. One of the women, standing in the middle of the stream, reached out and lent her a helping hand.

Reaching the bank, she took off her shoes and began to wade across. The women on the farther bank stood watching her hazardous progress with blank amazement.

She caught hold of Shinji's mother's sleeve and made a clumsy attempt at private conversation, whispering words into her ear that everyone around could plainly hear.

"Maybe this isn't quite the place, but I've been wanting to ask how things have gotten on for Shinji-san and Hatsue-san lately."

The suddenness of the question made the other's eyes grow round, and she said nothing.

"Shinji-san likes Hatsue-san, doesn't he?"

"Well—"

"And still Terukichi-san is standing in the way, isn't he?"

"Well—that's what the trouble is all right, but . . ."

"And how does Hatsue-san feel about it?"

At this point the other divers, who could not have helped overhearing, broke into the private conversation. Where talk of Hatsue was concerned all the divers without exception had become her staunch defenders ever since that day when the peddler had held the contest. They had also heard the whole true story from Hatsue herself and were one and all against Terukichi.

"Hatsue—she's head over heels in love with Shinji too. That's the plain truth of it, mistress. And yet, would you believe it, that Uncle Teru is planning to marry her to that good-for-nothing Yasuo! Have you ever heard of such foolishness?"

"Well, that's that," said the mistress of the lighthouse, as though addressing a classroom of students. "Today I received a threatening letter from my daughter in Tokyo saying she didn't know what she might do if I wouldn't help get the two married. So I'm on my way to have a talk with Terukichi-san, but I thought I ought to stop and find out how Shinji-san's mother felt about it first."

Shinji's mother reached down and picked up her son's sleeping kimono, which she had been treading clean beneath her feet. Slowly she proceeded to wring it out, gaining time for thought. Finally she turned to face the mistress of the lighthouse and bowed her head low.

"I'll greatly appreciate anything you can do," she said.

Moved by a spirit of helpfulness, the other women went into noisy conclave with each other, like a flock of water fowl beside a river, and decided that if they went along too as representatives of the women of the village, the show of strength might help awe Terukichi. The mistress of the lighthouse agreed, so the five of them, not including Shinji's mother, wrung out their washing hurriedly and ran to take it home, arranging to meet at the bend of the road leading to Terukichi's house.

The mistress of the lighthouse stood just inside the gloomy earthen-floored room of the Miyata house.

"Good day!" she called in a voice still youthful and steady.

There was no answer.

The other five women stood just outside the door, their sunburned faces thrusting forward like so many cactus leaves, their eyes glittering with enthusiasm as they peered into the dark interior.

The mistress of the lighthouse called out again, her voice echoing emptily through the house.

Presently the staircase gave a squeak and Terukichi himself came down wearing an undress kimono. Hatsue was apparently not at home.

"Why, it's Mistress Lighthouse-Keeper," Terukichi grumbled, standing imposingly on the threshold leading up from the earthen floor.

Most visitors at this house felt the urge to flee when received by this perpetually inhospitable visage with its bristling mane of white hair. The mistress herself was daunted, but she drummed up courage to continue:

"There's something I'd like to talk with you about for a minute."

"So? All right, please come in."

Terukichi turned his back and promptly went up the stairs. She followed him, with the other five women tiptoeing after her.

Terukichi led the way into the inner sitting-room upstairs and, without further ceremony, took the seat of honor in front of the alcove for himself. His face revealed no great surprise when he noticed the number of visitors in the room had grown to six. Ignoring them all, he looked toward the open windows. His hands were toying with a fan showing a picture of a beautiful woman advertising a drugstore in Toba.

The windows looked out directly over the island's harbor. There was only one vessel inside the breakwater, a boat belonging to the Co-operative. Far in the distance summer clouds were floating over the Gulf of Ise.

The sunshine outdoors was so brilliant that it made the room seem dark. On the alcove wall there hung a calligraphic scroll done by the last-governor-but-one of Mie Prefecture, and beneath it, gleaming with a luster like that of wax, there were an ornamental rooster and its hen, their bodies carved out of a knotty and gnarled root of a tree and their tails and combs formed from the natural growth of the slender shoots.

The mistress of the lighthouse sat at this side of the bare rosewood table. The other five women, having mislaid somewhere their courage of a little while before, now sat primly just in front of the bamboo blind hanging in the entrance to the room, as though they were giving an exhibit of housedresses.

Terukichi continued looking out the window and did not open his mouth.

The sultry silence of a summer afternoon came upon them, broken only by the buzzing of several large bluebottle flies that were flying about the room.

The mistress of the lighthouse wiped the sweat from her face several times. At long last she began to speak:

"Well, what I want to talk to you about is your Hatsue-san and the Kubo family's Shinji-san, and . . ."

Terukichi was still looking out the window. After a long pause he spoke, seeming to spit out the words:

"Hatsue and Shinji?"

"Yes . . ."

Now for the first time Terukichi turned his face toward her, and then he spoke, without so much as a sign of a smile:

"If that's all you have to talk about, it's all already settled. Shinji's the one I'm adopting for Hatsue's husband."

There was a stir among the women as though a dam had burst. But Terukichi went right on speaking, paying not the slightest heed to his visitors' reaction:

"But in any case they're still too young, so for the time being I've decided to leave it at an engagement, and then, after Shinji comes of age, we'll have a proper ceremony. I hear his old lady isn't having too easy a time of it, so I'll be willing to take both her and the younger brother in, or, depending upon how it's finally decided, help them out with some money each month. I haven't said anything to anybody about all this yet, though.

"I was angry at first, but then, after I made them stop seeing each other, Hatsue became so out of sorts that I decided things couldn't go on that way. So I decided on a plan. I gave Shinji and Yasuo berths on my ship and told the captain to watch and see which one of them made the best showing. I let the captain tell all this to Jukichi as a secret, and I don't suppose Jukichi has told Shinji even yet. Well, anyway, to make a short story of it, the captain really fell in love with Shinji and decided I'd never be able to find a better husband for Hatsue. And then when Shinji did that great thing at Okinawa—well, I changed my mind too and decided he was the one for my girl. The only thing that really counts . . ."

Here Terukichi raised his voice emphatically.

"The only thing that really counts in a man is his get-up-and-go. If he's got get-up-and-go he's a real man, and those are the kind of men we need here on Uta-jima. Family and money are all secondary. Don't you think so, Mistress Lighthouse-Keeper? And that's what he's got—Shinji—get-up-and-go."

# 16

Shinji could now visit the Miyata house openly. One night after returning from fishing he called Hatsue's name from the front door. He was wearing freshly laundered trousers and a clean white sport shirt, and from each hand there dangled a big red-snapper.

Hatsue was ready and waiting. They had made a date to go to Yashiro Shrine and the lighthouse to announce their engagement and express their thanks.

The dusk in the earthen-floored room became lighter when Hatsue entered. She was wearing the light summer kimono with large-patterned morning-glories on a white background that she had bought on that occasion from the peddler, and its whiteness was brilliant even at night.

Shinji had been leaning against the door waiting, but when Hatsue came out he suddenly looked down, waved one clog-shod foot as though to drive away insects, and mumbled:

"The mosquitoes are terrible."

"Aren't they though?"

They went up the stone stairs leading to Yashiro Shrine. They could easily have run up them at a single breath, but instead, their hearts filled to overflowing with contentment, they ascended slowly, as though savoring the pleasure of each separate step. When they reached the hundredth step, they paused as though reluctant to end this happy climb by going on to the top. The boy wanted to hold her hand, but the red-snappers prevented him.

Nature too again smiled on them. When they reached the top they turned around and looked out over the Gulf of Ise. The night sky was filled with stars and, as for clouds, there was only a low bank stretching across the horizon in the direction of the Chita Peninsula, through which soundless lightning ran from time to time. Nor was the sound of the waves strong, but coming regularly and peacefully, as though the sea were breathing in healthy slumber.

Passing through the pine grove, they reached the unpretentious shrine and stopped to worship. The boy was filled with pride by the loud and clear sound his formal handclap made, ringing out far and wide. So he clapped his hands again.

Hatsue had bowed her head and was praying. Against the white background of her kimono collar, the nape of her suntanned neck did not look particularly white, and yet it charmed Shinji more than the whitest of white necks could have done.

In his heart the boy reminded himself again of his happiness—the gods had indeed given him everything he had prayed for.

They prayed for a long while. And, in the very fact of their never once having doubted the providence of the gods, they could feel that providence around them.

The shrine office was brightly lit. Shinji called out and the priest came to the window.

Shinji's words were rather vague, and for a while the priest could make neither head nor tail of what the two had come about. But at last he understood, and Shinji presented him with one of the red-snappers as their offering to the gods. Receiving this splendid gift from the sea, the priest was reminded that presently he would be officiating at their wedding rites. He congratulated them heartily.

Climbing the path through the pine grove behind the shrine, they again savored the night's coolness. Though the sun was completely set, the cicadas were still singing. The path leading up to the lighthouse was steep. One of his hands was now free, so Shinji held the girl's hand.

"Me," said Shinji, "I'm thinking I'll take the exam and get a first mate's license. You can after you're twenty, you know."

"Oh, that'd be wonderful."

"If I got my license, I guess it'd be all right to have the wedding then."

Hatsue made no reply but only smiled shyly.

They rounded Woman's Slope and approached the residence of the lighthouse-keeper. The boy called out his greetings as always at the glass door, where they could again see the mistress's shadow moving about as she prepared supper.

The mistress opened the door. There in the darkness she saw the boy and his betrothed standing hesitantly.

"Oh, here you both are, and welcome," the wife called out in a loud voice, finally taking in both hands the large fish that was thrust out to her. Then she called back into the house:

"Father, here's Shinji-san with a fine red-snapper for us."

Taking his ease in one of the inner rooms, the lighthouse-keeper called back without getting up:

"Thanks as always. And this time it's congratulations too. Come in, come in."

"Please do come in," the mistress added. "Tomorrow Chiyoko's coming back, too."

The boy had not the slightest idea of all the emotions he had aroused in Chiyoko, nor of the mental anguish she had experienced because of him, and he heard the mother's abrupt remark without attaching any significance to it.

Having been almost forcibly made to stay for supper, they stayed on for nearly an hour longer, and then it was decided that the lighthouse-keeper would show them around the lighthouse on their way home. Hatsue, having only recently returned to the island, had never seen the interior of the lighthouse.

First the lighthouse-keeper showed them the watch-house. To reach it from the residence they walked along the edge of the small vegetable garden, where radishes had been planted just the day before, and climbed a flight of concrete steps. At the top there was the lighthouse, standing back against the mountain, and the watchhouse at the edge of the cliff that fell to the sea.

The beacon of the lighthouse, like a shining column of fog, was sweeping from right to left across the top of the watchhouse gable on the side facing the sea. The lighthouse-keeper opened the door of the watchhouse and, preceding them, turned on a light. They saw the drafting triangles hanging on a window frame, the scrupulously tidy desk with its log for recording ships' movements, and, on a tripod facing the windows, the telescope.

The lighthouse-keeper opened a window, adjusted the telescope, and lowered it to the right height for Hatsue.

Hatsue took one look through the telescope, stopped and wiped the lens with her kimono sleeve, looked again, and gave a shout of joy:

"Oh, beautiful!"

Then, as Hatsue pointed to the lights in various directions, Shinji picked them out with his phenomenally keen eyes and explained them to her.

Keeping her eye to the telescope, Hatsue pointed first to the scores of lights dotting the sea to the southeast.

"Those? They're the lights of the drag-net boats. They come from over in Aichi Prefecture."

It seemed as though each of the vast number of lights out over the sea found its counterpart somewhere among the vast number of stars in the sky. Directly opposite was the beam from the lighthouse on Cape Irako. Behind it were scattered the lights of the town of Cape Irako, and to the left the lights of Shino Island were faintly visible.

At their extreme left they could see the Cape Noma lighthouse on the Chita Peninsula. To its right were the clustered lights of the port of Toyohama. That red light in the middle—that was the light on the port's breakwater. And, far to the right, there flickered the aircraft beacon on top of Mt. Oyama.

Hatsue gave a second cry of admiration. A large ocean-liner had just come into the field of the telescope. It was scarcely visible to the naked eye, but as the ship made its stately way across the telescope's field of view, its deli-cate reflection was so splendid and clear that the boy and girl compromised by taking turns at the telescope.

It seemed to be a combined cargo and passenger ship of two or three thousand tons. In a room off the promenade deck they could plainly see several tables spread with white cloths, and a number of chairs. Not a single person was visible. The room was apparently the dining-salon, and as they were examining its walls of white asphalt-tile, suddenly a white-uniformed steward entered from the right and passed in front of the windows. . . .

Presently the vessel, carrying green lights at bow and stern, passed out of the telescope's range and sailed away through the Irako Channel, bound for the Pacific.

The lighthouse-keeper took them next to the light-house itself. On the ground floor the electric generator was making a rumbling noise, surrounded by the odor of oil—oil cans, oil lamps, and tins of oil. Ascending the nar-row spiral staircase, they found, housed in a small and lonely round room at the top, the source of the light-house's light, living its life away in silence.

Looking from the window, they watched the beam of light making its vast sweeps from right to left across the black, clamoring waves of the Irako Channel.

Tactfully, the lighthouse-keeper went back down the spiral staircase, leaving the two of them alone there.

• • •

The small round room at the top of the tower was enclosed in walls of polished wood. Its brass fittings gleaming, the thick glass lens revolved leisurely around the five-hundred-watt electric bulb, magnifying this source of light to sixty-five thousand candle power and maintaining a speed that produced a constant series of flashes. Reflections from the lens moved around the circular wooden wall and, to the accompaniment of the squeak-squeak-squeak revolving sound characteristic of lighthouses built before the turn of the century, these same reflections played across the backs of the boy and his betrothed, who had their faces pressed against the window.

They felt their cheeks so close together that they could touch at any moment, felt too the flaming heat of each other's cheeks. . . . Out in front of them stretched the unfathomable darkness, where the beam from the lighthouse was making its vast, regular sweeps. And the reflections of the lens kept circling around inside the little room, their patterns disrupted only at the spot where they crossed the backs of the white shirt and the flower-patterned kimono.

Once again it came to pass that Shinji, little given to thinking as he was, was lost in thought. He was thinking that in spite of all they'd been through, here they were in the end, free within the moral code to which they had been born, never once having been estranged from the providence of the gods . . . that, in short, it was this little island, enfolded in darkness, that had protected their happiness and brought their love to this fulfillment. . . .

Suddenly Hatsue turned to Shinji and laughed. From

her sleeve she took out a small, pink shell and showed it to him.

"Remember this?"

"I remember."

The boy flashed his beautiful teeth in a smile. Then, from the breast pocket of his shirt, he took out the snapshot of Hatsue and showed it to her.

Hatsue touched the picture lightly with her own hand and then returned it. Her eyes were full of pride. She was thinking it was her picture that had protected Shinji.

But at this moment Shinji lifted his eyebrows. He knew it had been his own strength that had tided him through that perilous night.

### FIVE MODERN NŌ PLAYS

Japanese Nō drama is one of the world's great art forms. Yukio Mishima, one of Japan's outstanding postwar writers, infused new life into the form by using it for plays that preserve the style and inner spirit of Nō but are at the same time so modern, so direct, and intelligible that they could, as he suggested, be played on a bench in Central Park. Here are five of his Nō plays, stunning in their contemporary nature and relevance—and finally made available again for readers to enjoy.

Drama

### FORBIDDEN COLORS

From one of Japan's greatest modern writers comes an exquisitely disturbing novel of sexual combat and concealed passion, a work that distills beauty, longing, and loathing into an intoxicating poisoned cocktail. An aging, embittered novelist sets out to avenge himself on the women who have betrayed him. He finds the perfect instrument in Yuichi, a young man whose beauty makes him irresistible to women but who is just discovering his attraction to other men. As Yuichi's mentor presses him into a loveless marriage and a series of equally loveless philanderings, his protégé enters the gay underworld of postwar Japan. In that hidden society of parks and tearooms, prostitutes and aristocratic blackmailers, Yuichi is as defenseless as any of the women he preys on. Mordantly observed, intellectually provocative, and filled with icy eroticism, *Forbidden Colors* is a masterpiece.

Fiction

Thirteen-year-old Noboru is a member of a gang of highly philosophical teenage boys who reject the tenets of the adult world—to them, adult life is illusory, hypocritical, and sentimental. When Noboru's widowed mother is romanced by Ryuji, a sailor, Noboru is thrilled. He idolizes this rugged man of the sea as a hero. But his admiration soon turns to hatred as Ryuji forsakes life onboard the ship for marriage, rejecting everything Noboru holds sacred. Upset and appalled, he and his friends respond to this apparent betrayal with a terrible ferocity.

Fiction

ALSO AVAILABLE

*After the Banquet*
*The Temple of the Golden Pavillion*
*Thirst for Love*

*The Sea of Fertility*

*Spring Snow*
*Runaway Horses*
*The Temple of Dawn*
*The Decay of the Angel*

VINTAGE INTERNATIONAL
Available wherever books are sold.
www.vintagebooks.com